W9-CMT-671

Chronicles of a Comer
and Other Religious
Science Fiction Stories

chronicles of a comer and other religious science fiction stories

EDITED BY ROGER ELWOOD

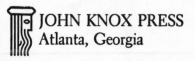

JOHN KNOX PRESS
Atlanta, Georgia

For material previously published elsewhere, the following credits are given:

"The Problem of Pain" by Poul Anderson. © 1973 by Mercury Press. From *Fantasy and Science Fiction*. Reprinted by permission of author and author's agent.

"The Wolfram Hunters" by Edward D Hoch. Reprinted by permission of the author and the author's agent, Larry Sternig.

"The Gift of Nothing" by Joan C. Holly. © 1972 by Joan C. Holly. Reprinted by permission of the author.

"Towards the Beloved City" by Philip José Farmer. © 1972 Fleming H. Revell Company. Reprinted by permission of the author and the author's agent, Scott Meredith Literary Agency.

"Chronicles of a Comer" by K. M. O'Donnell. © 1972 by K. M. O'Donnell. Reprinted by permission of the author.

"In This Sign" by Ray Bradbury. © 1951 by Ray Bradbury. From *Imagination* magazine. Reprinted by permission of the author and the author's agent, Harold Matson Company.

Library of Congress Cataloging in Publication Data

Elwood, Roger, comp.
   Chronicles of a comer, and other religious science fiction stories.

   CONTENTS: Anderson, P. The problem of pain.—Hoch, E. D. The wolfram hunters.—Holly, J. C. The gift of nothing. [etc.]
   1. Science fiction, American. I. Title.
PZ1.E49Ch [PS648.S3]   813'.0876   73-16910
ISBN 0-8042-1933-8

© John Knox Press 1974
Printed in the United States of America

PZ1
.E52
1974
Scots

contents

foreword

The heritage of religious themes woven into the fabric of superior science fiction goes back quite far in the development of the genre. H. G. Wells' *War of the Worlds* concluded that nothing created by men could stem the Martian attacks; only God could do that; ironically enough, the smallest of his creatures, microbes, did the job, infecting the defenseless somatic systems of the invading aliens with dramatic—and, for us, humbling—effectiveness.

Even Mary W. Shelley's *Frankenstein* carried with it the warning that once man attempts to trespass into God's domain—in this case, creating or resurrecting life—it is quite certain that his vengeance will soon follow.

More modern science fiction—never call the genre *sci-fi*; purists hate that term with a real passion—has dabbled in religious themes again and again, and, coincidentally or not, this has resulted in some of the abiding classics: Arthur C. Clarke's *Childhood's End*, Walter M. Miller, Jr.'s *Canticle for Leibowitz*, James Blish's *Case of Conscience*, and so on. Could it be said that the themes of God, sin, and redemption bring out the best in science fiction authors?

The stories of which this anthology are comprised are all religious in theme, and at least partially Christian in orientation. Four of the authors included are among the most prominent in the genre: K. M. O'Donnell, Poul Anderson, Ray Bradbury, and Philip José Farmer. The two other authors are less well known but more than capable: Edward D Hoch and Joan C. Holly.

Farmer's *Towards the Beloved City* is probably the most Biblically oriented of all, and perhaps the most theologically complex. Farmer deals with the tribulation in an exciting, accurate, incisive manner.

Anderson's *Problem of Pain* deals with such issues as pantheism, atheism, and the importance of conscience.

Holly's *Gift of Nothing* is concerned with what happens to an alien race when its beliefs clash with those of earthmen.

The other stories are equally interesting, with plots concerned with personal issues and social implications and eschatological motifs rather than bug-eyed monsters or whizzing spaceships.

Over the past three years I have edited more than eighty anthologies of science fiction. It is my intention to show how the best of science fiction makes us aware of the moral and spiritual dimensions of our universe. This anthology is a start toward reader-awareness of religious science fiction. I hope you like the stories herein.

ROGER ELWOOD

Chronicles of a Comer
and Other Religious
Science Fiction Stories

the problem of pain

BY POUL ANDERSON

Maybe only a Christian can understand this story. In that case, I don't qualify. But I do take an interest in religion, as part of being an amateur psychologist, and—for the grandeur of its language if nothing else—a Bible is among the reels that accompany me wherever I go. This was one reason Peter Berg told me what had happened in his past. He desperately needed to make sense of it, and no priest he'd talked to had quite laid his questions to rest. There was an outside chance that an outside viewpoint like mine would see what a man couldn't who was within the faith.

His other reason was simple loneliness. We were on Lucifer, as part of a study corporation. That world is well named. It will never be a real colony for any beings whose ancestors evolved amidst clean green-ery. But it might be marginally habitable, and if so, its mineral wealth would be worth exploiting. Our job was to determine whether that was true. The gentlest looking environment holds a thousand death traps until you have learned what the difficulties are and how to grip them. (Earth is no exception.) Sometimes you find problems which can't be solved economically, or can't be solved at all. Then you write off the area or the entire planet, and look for another.

We'd contracted to work three standard years on Lucifer. The pay was munificent, but presently we realized that no bank account could buy back one day we might have spent beneath a kindlier sun. It was a knowledge we carefully avoided discussing with teammates.

About midway through, Peter Berg and I were assigned to do an in-depth investigation of a unique cycle in the ecology of the northern middle latitudes. This meant that we settled down for weeks—which ran into months—in a sample region, well away from everybody else to minimize human disturbances. An occasional supply flitter gave us our only real contact; electronics were no proper substitute, especially when that hell-violent star was forever disrupting them.

Under such circumstances, you come to know your partner maybe better than you know yourself. Pete and I got along well. He's a big, sandy-haired, freckle-faced young man, altogether dependable, with enough kindliness, courtesy, and dignity that he need not make a show of them. Soft-spoken, he's a bit short in the humor department. Otherwise I recommend him as a companion. He has a lot to tell from his own wanderings, yet he'll listen with genuine interest to your memories and brags; he's well-read too, a good cook when his turn comes; he plays chess at just about my level of skill.

I already knew he wasn't from Earth, had in fact never been there, but from Aeneas, nearly 200 light-years distant, more than 300 from Lucifer. And, while he's gotten an education at the new little university in Nova Roma, he was raised in the outback. Besides, that town is only a far-off colonial capital. It helped explain his utter commitment to belief in a God who became flesh and died for love of man. Not that I scoff. When he said his prayers, night and morning in our one-room shelterdome, trustingly as a child, I didn't rag him nor he reproach me. Of course, over the weeks, we came more and more to talk about such matters.

At last he told me of that which haunted him.

We'd been out through the whole of one of Lucifer's long, long days; we'd toiled, we'd sweated, we'd itched and stunk and gotten grimy and staggered from weariness, we'd come near death once: and we'd found the uranium-concentrating root which was the key to the whole weirdness around us. We came back to base as day's fury was dying in the usual twilight gale; we washed, ate something, went to sleep with the hiss of storm-blown dust for a lullaby. Ten or twelve hours later we awoke and saw, through the vitryl panels, stars cold and crystalline beyond this thin air, auroras aflame, landscape hoar, and the twisted things we called trees all sheathed in glittering ice.

"Nothing we can do now till dawn," I said, "and we've earned a celebration." So we prepared a large meal, elaborate as possible—break-fast or supper, what relevance had that here? We drank wine in the course of it, and afterward much brandy while we sat, side by side in our loungers, watching the march of constellations which Earth never saw. And we talked. Finally we talked of God.

"—Maybe you can give me an idea," Pete said. In the dim light, his face bore a struggle. He stared before him and knotted his fingers.

"M-m, I dunno," I said carefully. "To be honest, no offense meant, theological conundrums strike me as silly."

He gave me a direct blue look. His tone was soft: "That is, you feel the paradoxes don't arise if we don't insist on believing?"

"Yes. I respect your faith, Pete, but it's not mine. And if I did suppose that a, well, a spiritual principle or something is behind the universe—" I gestured at the high and terrible sky—"in the name of reason, can we confine, can we understand whatever made *that*, in the bounds of one little dogma?"

"No. Agreed. How could finite minds grasp the infinite? We can see parts of it, though, that've been revealed to us." He drew breath. " 'Way back before space travel, the Church decided Jesus had come only to Earth, to man. If other intelligent races need salvation—and obviously a lot of them do!—God will have made His suitable arrangements for them. Sure. However, this does not mean Christianity is not true, or that certain different beliefs are not false."

"Like, say, polytheism, wherever you find it?"

"I think so. Besides, religions evolve. The primitive faiths see God, or the gods, as power; the higher ones see Him as justice; the highest see Him as love." Abruptly he fell silent. I saw his fist clench, until he grabbed up his glass and drained it and refilled it in nearly a single savage motion.

"I must believe that," he whispered.

I waited a few seconds, in Lucifer's crackling night stillness, before saying: "An experience made you wonder?"

"Made me . . . disturbed. Mind if I tell you?"

"Certainly not." I saw he was about to open himself; and I may be an unbeliever, but I know what is sacred.

"Happened about five years ago. I was on my first real job. So was the—" his voice stumbled the least bit—"the wife I had then. We were fresh out of school and apprenticeship, fresh into marriage. Our employers weren't human. They were Ythrians. Ever heard of them?"

I sought through my head. The worlds, races, beings are unknowably many, in this tiny corner of this one dust-mote galaxy which we have begun to explore a little. "Ythrians, Ythrians . . . wait. Do they fly?"

"Yes. Surely one of the most glorious sights in creation. Your Ythrian isn't as heavy as a man, of course; adults mass around twenty-five or thirty kilos—but his wingspan goes up to six meters, and when he soars with those feathers shining gold-grown in the light, or stoops in a crack of thunder and whistle of wind—"

"Hold on," I said. "I take it Ythri's a terrestroid planet?"

"Pretty much. Somewhat smaller and drier than Earth, somewhat thinner atmosphere—about like Aeneas, in fact, which it's not too far from as interstellar spaces go. You can live there without special protection. The biochemistry's quite similar to ours."

"Then how the devil can those creatures be that size? The wing loading's impossible, when you have only cell tissue to oxidize for power. They'd never get off the ground."

"Ah, but they have antlibranchs as well." Pete smiled, though it didn't go deep. "Those look like three gills, sort of, on either side, below the wings. They're actually more like bellows, pumped by the wing muscles. Extra oxygen is forced directly into the bloodstream during flight. A biological supercharger system."

"Well, I'll be a . . . never mind what." I considered, in delight, this new facet of nature's inventiveness. "Um-m-m . . . if they spend energy at that rate, they've got to have appetites to match."

"Right. They're carnivores. A number of them are still hunters. The advanced societies are based on ranching. In either case, obviously, it takes a lot of meat animals, a lot of square kilometers, to support one Ythrian. So they're fiercely territorial. They live in small groups—single families or extended households—which attack, with intent to kill, any uninvited outsider who doesn't obey an order to leave."

"And still they're civilized enough to hire humans for space exploration?"

"Uh-huh. Remember, being flyers, they've never needed to huddle in cities in order to have ready communication. They do keep a few towns, mining or manufacturing centers, but those are inhabited mostly by wing-clipped slaves. I'm glad to say that institution's dying out as they get modern machinery."

"By trade?" I guessed.

"Yes," Pete replied. "When the first Grand Survey discovered them, their most advanced culture was at an Iron Age level of technology; no industrial revolution, but a lot of sophisticated minds around, and subtle philosophies." He paused. "That's important to my question —that the Ythrians, at least of the Planha-speaking *choths*, are not barbarians and have not been for many centuries. They've had their equivalents of Socrates, Aristotle, Confucius, Galileo, yes, and their prophets and seers."

After another mute moment: "They realized early what the visitors from Earth implied, and set about attracting traders and teachers. Once they had some funds, they sent their promising young folk off-planet to study. I met several at my own university, which is why I got my job offer. By now they have a few spacecraft and native crews. But you'll understand, their technical people are spread thin, and in several branches of knowledge they have no experts. So they employ humans."

He went on to describe the typical Ythrian: warm-blooded, feathered like a golden eagle (though more intricately) save for a crest on the head, and yet not a bird. Instead of a beak, a blunt muzzle full of fangs juts before two great eyes. The female bears her young alive. While she does not nurse them, they have lips to suck the juices of meat and fruits, wherefore their speech is not hopelessly unlike man's. What were formerly the legs have evolved into arms bearing three taloned fingers, flanked by two thumbs, on each hand. Aground, the huge wings fold downward and, with the help of claws at the angles, give locomotion. That is slow and awkward—but aloft, ah!

"They become more alive, flying, than we ever do," Pete murmured. His gaze had lost itself in the shuddering auroras overhead. "They must: the metabolic rate they have then, and the space around them, speed, sky, a hundred winds to ride on and be kissed by.... That's what made me think Enherrian, in particular, believed more keenly than I could hope to. I saw him and others dancing, high, high in the air, swoops, glides, hoverings, sunshine molten on their plumes; I asked what they did, and was told they were honoring God."

He sighed. "Or that's how I translated the Planha phrase, rightly or wrongly," he went on. "Olga and I had taken a cram course, and our Ythrian teammates all knew Anglic; but nobody's command of the foreign tongue was perfect. It couldn't be. Multiple billion years of separate existence, evolution, history—what a miracle that we could think as alike as we did!

"However, you could call Enherrian religious, same as you could call me that, and not be too grotesquely off the mark. The rest varied, just like humans. Some were also devout, some less, some agnostics or atheists; two were pagans, following the bloody rites of what was called the Old Faith. For that matter, my Olga—" the knuckles stood forth where he grasped his tumbler of brandy—"had tried, for my sake, to believe as I did, and couldn't.

"Well. The New Faith interested me more. It was new only by comparison—at least half as ancient as mine. I hoped for a chance to study it, to ask questions and compare ideas. I really knew nothing except that it was monotheistic, had sacraments and a theology though no official priesthood, upheld a high ethical and moral standard—for Ythrians, I mean. You can't expect a race which can only live by killing animals, and has an oestrous cycle, and is incapable by instinct of maintaining what we'd recognize as a true nation or government, and on and on—you can't expect them to resemble Christians much. God has given them a different message. I wished to know what. Surely we could learn from it." Again he paused. "After all . . . being a faith with a long tradition . . . and not static but a seeking, a history of prophets and saints and believers . . . I thought it must know God is love. Now what form would God's love take to an Ythrian?"

He drank. I did too, before asking cautiously: "Uh, where was this expedition?"

Pete stirred in his lounger. "To a system about eighty light-years from Ythri's," he answered. "The original survey crew had discovered a terrestroid planet there. They didn't bother to name it. Prospective colonists would choose their own name anyway. Those could be human or Ythrian, conceivably both—if the environment proved out.

"Offhand, the world—our group called it, unofficially, Gray, after that old captain—the world looked brilliantly promising. It's intermediate in size between Earth and Ythri, surface gravity 0.8 terrestrial;

slightly more irradiation, from a somewhat yellower sun, than Earth gets, which simply makes it a little warmer; axial tilt, therefore seasonal variations, a bit less than terrestrial; length of year about three-quarters of ours, length of day a bit under half; one small, close-in, bright moon; biochemistry similar to ours—we could eat most native things, though we'd require imported crops and livestock to supplement the diet. All in all, seemingly well-nigh perfect."

"Rather remote to attract Earthlings at this early date," I remarked. "And from your description, the Ythrians won't be able to settle it for quite a while either."

"They think ahead," Pete responded. "Besides, they have scientific curiosity and, yes, in them perhaps even more than in the humans who went along, a spirit of adventure. Oh, it was a wonderful thing to be young in that band!"

He had not yet reached thirty, but somehow his cry was not funny.

He shook himself. "Well, we had to make sure," he said. "Besides planetology, ecology, chemistry, oceanography, meteorology, a million and a million mysteries to unravel for their own sakes—we must scout out the death traps, whatever those might be.

"At first everything went like Mary's smile on Christmas morning. The spaceship set us off—it couldn't be spared to linger in orbit—and we established base on the largest continent. Soon our hundred-odd dispersed across the globe, investigating this or that. Olga and I made part of a group on the southern shore, where a great gulf swarmed with life. A strong current ran eastward from there, eventually striking an archipelago which deflected it north. Flying over those waters, we spied immense, I mean immense patches—no, floating islands—of vegetation, densely interwoven, grazed on by monstrous marine creatures, no doubt supporting any number of lesser plant and animal species.

"We wanted a close look. Our camp's sole aircraft wasn't good for that. Anyhow, it was already in demand for a dozen jobs. We had boats, though, and launched one. Our crew was Enherrian, his wife Whell, their grown children Rusa and Arrach, my beautiful new bride Olga, and me. We'd take three or four Gray days to reach the nearest atlantis weed, as Olga dubbed it. Then we'd be at least a week exploring before we turned back—a vacation, a lark, a joy."

He tossed off his drink and reached for the bottle. "You ran into grief," I prompted.

"No." He bent his lips upward, stiffly. "It ran into us. A hurricane. Unpredicted; we knew very little about that planet. Given the higher solar energy input and, especially, the rapid rotation, the storm was more violent than would've been possible on Earth. We could only run and pray.

"At least, I prayed, and imagined that Enherrian did."

Wind shrieked, hooted, yammered, hit flesh with fists and cold knives. Waves rumbled in that driven air, black and green and fang-white, fading from view as the sun sank behind the cloud-roil which hid it. Often a monster among them loomed castle-like over the gunwale. The boat slipped by, spilled into the troughs, rocked onto the crests and down again. Spindrift, icy, stinging, bitter on lips and tongue, made a fog across her length.

"We'll live if we can keep sea room," Enherrian had said when the fury first broke. "She's well-found. The engine capacitors have ample kilowatt-hours in them. Keep her bow on and we'll live."

But the currents had them now, where the mighty gulf stream met the outermost islands and its waters churned, recoiled, spun about and fought. Minute by minute, the riptides grew wilder. They made her yaw till she was broadside on and surges roared over her deck; they shocked her onto her beam ends, and the hull became a toning bell.

Pete, Olga, and Whell were in the cabin, trying to rest before their next watch. That was no longer possible. The Ythrian female locked hands and wing-claws around the net-covered framework wherein she had slept, hung on and uttered nothing. In the wan glow of a single overhead fluoro, among thick restless shadows, her eyes gleamed topaz. They did not seem to look at the crampedness around—at what, then?

The humans had secured themselves by a line onto a lower bunk. They embraced, helping each other fight the leaps and swings which tried to smash them against the sides. Her fair hair on his shoulder was the last brightness in his cosmos. "I love you," she said, over and over, through hammer blows and groans. "Whatever happens, I love you, Pete, I thank you for what you've given me."

"And you," he would answer. *And You*, he would think. *Though*

You won't take her, not yet, will You? Me, yes, if that's Your Will. But not Olga. It'd leave Your creation too dark.

A wing smote the cabin door. Barely to be heard through the storm, an Ythrian voice—high, whistly, but resonant out of full lungs—shouted: "Come topside!"

Whell obeyed at once, the Bergs as fast as they could slip on life jackets. Having taken no personal grav units along, they couldn't fly free if they went overboard. Dusk raved around them. Pete could just see Rusa and Arrach in the stern, fighting the tiller. Enherrian stood before him and pointed forward. "Look," the captain said. Pete, who had no nictitating membranes, must shield his eyes with fingers to peer athwart the hurricane. He saw a deeper darkness hump up from a wall of white; he heard surf crash.

"We can't pull free," Enherrian told him. "Between wind and current—too little power. We'll likely be wrecked. Make ready."

Olga's hand went briefly to her mouth. She huddled against Pete and might have whispered, "Oh, no." Then she straightened, swung back down into the cabin, braced herself as best she could, and started assembling the most vital things. He saw that he loved her still more than he had known.

The same calm descended on him. Nobody had time to be afraid. He got busy too. The Ythrians could carry a limited weight of equipment and supplies—but sharply limited under these conditions. The humans, buoyed by their jackets, must carry most. They strapped it to their bodies.

When they re-emerged, the boat was in the shoals. Enherrian ordered them to take the rudder. His wife, son, and daughter stood around—on hands which clutched the rails with prey-snatching strength—and spread their wings to give a bit of shelter. The captain clung to the cabin top as lookout. His yelled commands reached the Bergs dim, tattered.

"Hard right!" Upward cataracts burst on a skerry to port. It glided past, was lost in murk. "Two points starboard—steady!" The hull slipped between a pair of rocks. Ahead was a narrow opening in the island's sheer black face. To a lagoon, to safety? Surf raged on either side of that gate, and everywhere else.

The passage was impossible. The boat struck, threw Olga off her feet and Arrach off her perch. Full reverse engine could not pull free. The deck canted. A billow and a billow smashed across.

Pete was in the water. It grabbed him, pulled him under, dragged him over a sharp bottom. He thought: *Into Your hands, God. Spare Olga, please, please*—and the sea spewed him back up for one gulp of air.

Wallowing in blindness, he tried to gauge how the breakers were acting, what he should do. If he could somehow belly-surf in, he might make it, he barely might. . . . He was on the neck of a rushing giant, it climbed and climbed, it shoved him forward at what he knew was lunatic speed. He saw the reef on which it was about to smash him and knew he was dead.

Talons closed on his jacket. Air brawled beneath wings. The Ythrian could not raise him, but could draw him aside . . . the bare distance needed, and Pete went past the rock whereon his bones were to have been crushed, down into the smother and chaos beyond. The Ythrian didn't break free in time. He glimpsed the plumes go under, as he himself did. They never rose.

He beat on, and on, without end.

He floated in water merely choppy, swart palisades to right and left, a slope of beach ahead. He peered into the clamorous dark and found nothing. "Olga," he croaked. "Olga. Olga."

Wings shadowed him among the shadows. "Get ashore before an undertow eats you!" Enherrian whooped, and beat his way off in search.

Pete crawled to gritty sand, fell, and let annihilation have him. He wasn't unconscious long. When he revived, Rusa and Whell were beside him. Enherrian was further inland. The captain hauled on a line he had snubbed around a tree. Olga floated at the other end. She had no strength left, but he had passed a bight beneath her arms and she was alive.

At wolf-gray dawn the wind had fallen to gale force or maybe less, and the cliffs shielded lagoon and strand from it. Overhead it shrilled, and outside the breakers cannonaded, their rage aquiver through the island. Pete and Olga huddled together, a shared cloak across their shoulders. Enherrian busied himself checking the salvaged material.

Whell sat on the hindbones of her wings and stared seaward. Moisture gleamed on her grizzled feathers like tears.

Rusa flew in from the reefs and landed. "No trace," he said. His voice was emptied by exhaustion. "Neither the boat nor Arrach." Through the rust in his own brain, Pete noticed the order of those words.

Nevertheless—He leaned toward the parents and brother of Arrach, who had been beautiful and merry and had sung to them by moonlight. "How can we say—?" he began, realized he didn't have Planha words, and tried in Anglic: "How can we say how sorry we both are?"

"No necessity," Rusa answered.

"She died saving me!"

"And what you were carrying, which we needed badly." Some energy returned to Rusa. He lifted his head and its crest. "She had deathpride, our lass."

Afterward Pete, in his search for meaning, would learn about that Ythrian concept. "Courage" is too simple and weak a translation. Certain Old Japanese words came closer, though they don't really bear the same value either.

Whell turned her hawk gaze full upon him. "Did you see anything of what happened in the water?" she asked. He was too unfamiliar with her folk to interpret the tone; today he thinks it was loving. He did know that, being creatures of seasonal rut, Ythrians are less sexually motivated than man is, but probably treasure their young even more. The strongest bond between male and female is children, who are what life is all about.

"No, I . . . I fear not," he stammered.

Enherrian reached out to lay claws, very gently and briefly, on his wife's back. "Be sure she fought well," he said. "She gave God honor." (Glory? Praise? Adoration? His due?)

Does he mean she prayed, made her confession, while she drowned? The question dragged itself through Pete's weariness and caused him to murmur: "She's in heaven now." Again he was forced to use Anglic words.

Enherrian gave him a look which he could have sworn was startled. "What do you say? Arrach is dead."

"Why, her . . . her spirit—"

"Will be remembered in pride." Enherrian resumed his work.

Olga said it for Pete: "So you don't believe the spirit outlives the body?"

"How could it?" Enherrian snapped. "Why should it?" His motions, his posture, the set of his plumage added: Leave me alone.

Pete thought: *Well, many faiths, including high ones, including some sects which call themselves Christian, deny immortality. How sorry I feel for these my friends, who don't know they will meet their beloved afresh!*

They will, regardless. It makes no sense that God, Who created what is because in His goodness He wished to share existence, would shape a soul only to break it and throw it away.

Never mind. The job on hand is to keep Olga alive, in her dear body. "Can I help?"

"Yes, check our medical kit," Enherrian said.

It had come through undamaged in its box. The items for human use—stimulants, sedatives, anesthetics, antitoxins, antibiotics, coagulants, healing promoters, et standard cetera—naturally outnumbered those for Ythrians. There hasn't been time to develop a large scientific pharmacopoeia for the latter species. True, certain materials work on both, as does the surgical and monitoring equipment. Pete distributed pills which took the pain out of bruises and scrapes, the heaviness out of muscles. Meanwhile Rusa collected wood, Whell started and tended a fire, Olga made breakfast. They had considerable food, mostly freeze-dried, gear to cook it, tools like knives and a hatchet, cord, cloth, flashbeams, two blasters and abundant recharges: what they required for survival.

"It may be insufficient," Enherrian said. "The portable radio transceiver went down with Arrach. The boat's transmitter couldn't punch a call through that storm, and now the boat's on the bottom—nothing to see from the air, scant metal to register on a detector."

"Oh, they'll check on us when the weather slacks off," Olga said. She caught Pete's hand in hers. He felt the warmth.

"If their flitter survived the hurricane, which I doubt," Enherrian stated. "I'm convinced the camp was also struck. We had built no

shelter for the flitter, our people will have been too busy saving themselves to secure it, and I think that thin shell was tumbled about and
broken. If I'm right, they'll have to call for an aircraft from elsewhere,
which may not be available at once. In either case, we could be anywhere
in a huge territory; and the expedition has no time or personnel for an
indefinite search. They will seek us, aye; however, if we are not found
before an arbitrary date—" A ripple passed over the feathers of face and
neck; a human would have shrugged.

"What . . . can we do?" the girl asked.

"Clear a sizable area in a plainly artificial pattern, or heap fuel for
beacon fires should a flitter pass within sight—whichever is practicable.
If nothing comes of that, we should consider building a raft or the like."

"Or modify a life jacket for me," Rusa suggested, "and I can try
to fly to the mainland."

Enherrian nodded. "We must investigate the possibilities. First
let's get a real rest."

The Ythrians were quickly asleep, squatted on their locked wing
joints like idols of a forgotten people. Pete and Olga felt more excited
and wandered a distance off, hand in hand.

Above the crag-enclosed beach, the island rose toward a crest
which he estimated as three kilometers away. If it was in the middle,
this was no large piece of real estate. Nor did he see adequate shelter.
A mat of mossy, intensely green plants squeezed out any possibility of
forest. A few trees stood isolated. Their branches tossed in the wind. He
noticed particularly one atop a great outcrop nearby, gaunt brown trunk
and thin leaf-fringed boughs that whipped insanely about. Blossoms,
torn from vines, flew past, and they were gorgeous; but there would be
naught to live on here, and he wasn't hopeful about learning, in time,
how to catch Gray's equivalent of fish.

"Strange about them, isn't it?" Olga murmured.

"Eh?" He came startled out of his preoccupations.

She gestured at the Ythrians. "Them. The way they took poor
Arrach's death."

"Well, you can't judge them by our standards. Maybe they feel
grief less than we would, or maybe their culture demands stoicism." He
looked at her and did not look away again. "To be frank, darling, I can't

really mourn either. I'm too happy to have you back."

"And I you—oh, Pete, Pete, my only—"

They found a secret spot and made love. He saw nothing wrong in that. Do you ever in this life come closer to the wonder which is God?

Afterward they returned to their companions. Thus the clash of wings awoke them, hours later. They scrambled from their bedrolls and saw the Ythrians swing aloft.

The wind was strong and loud as yet, though easing off in fickleness, flaws, downdrafts, whirls and eddies. Clouds were mostly gone. Those which remained raced gold and hot orange before a sun low in the west, across blue serenity. The lagoon glittered purple, the greensward lay aglow. It had warmed up till rich odors of growth, of flowers, blent with the sea-salt.

And splendid in the sky danced Enherrian, Whell, and Rusa. They wheeled, soared, pounced and rushed back into light which ran molten off their pinions. They chanted, and fragments blew down to the humans: *"High flew your spirit on many winds . . . be always remembered. . . ."*

"What *is* that?" Olga breathed.

"Why, they—they—" The knowledge broke upon Pete. "They're holding a service for Arrach."

He knelt and said a prayer for her soul's repose. But he wondered if she, who had belonged to the air, would truly want rest. And his eyes could not leave her kindred.

Enherrian screamed a hunter's challenge and rushed down at the earth. He flung himself meteoric past the stone outcrop Pete had seen; for an instant the man gasped, believing he would be shattered; then he rose, triumphant.

He passed by the lean tree of thin branches. Gusts flailed them about. A nearly razor edge took off his left wing. Blood spurted; Ythrian blood is royal purple. Somehow Enherrian slewed around and made a crash landing on the bluff top just beyond range of what has since been named the surgeon tree.

Pete yanked the medikit to him and ran. Olga wailed, briefly, and followed. When they reached the scene, they found that Whell and Rusa had pulled feathers from their breasts to try staunching the wound.

Evening, night, day, evening, night.

Enherrian sat before a campfire. Its light wavered, picked him red out of shadow and let him half vanish again, save for the unblinking yellow eyes. His wife and son supported him. Stim, cell-freeze, and plasma surrogate had done their work, and he could speak in a weak roughness. The bandages on his stump were a glaring white.

Around crowded shrubs which, by day, showed low and russet-leaved. They filled a hollow on the far side of the island, to which Enherrian had been carried in an improvised litter. Their odor was rank, in an atmosphere once more subtropically hot, and they clutched at feet with raking twigs. But this was the most sheltered spot his companions could find, and he might die in a new storm on the open beach.

He looked through smoke, at the Bergs, who sat as close together as they were able. He said—the surf growled faintly beneath his words, while never a leaf rustled in the breathless dark—"I have read that your people can make a lost part grow forth afresh."

Pete couldn't answer. He tried but couldn't. It was Olga who had the courage to say, "We can do it for ourselves. None except ourselves." She laid her head on her man's breast and wept.

Well, you need a lot of research to unravel a genetic code, a lot of development to make the molecules of heredity repeat what they did in the womb. Science hasn't had time yet for other races. It never will for all. They are too many.

"As I thought," Enherrian said. "Nor can a proper prosthesis be engineered in my lifetime. I have few years left; an Ythrian who cannot fly soon becomes sickly."

"Grav units—" Pete faltered.

The scorn in those eyes was like a blow. Dead metal to raise you, who have had wings?

Fierce and haughty though the Ythrian is, his quill-clipped slaves have never rebelled: for they are only half alive. Imagine yourself, human male, castrated. Enherrian might flap his remaining wing and the stump to fill his blood with air; but he would have nothing he could do with that extra energy, it would turn inward and corrode his body, perhaps at last his mind.

For a second, Whell laid an arm around him.

"You will devise a signal tomorrow," Enherrian said, "and start work on it. Too much time has already been wasted."

Before they slept, Pete managed to draw Whell aside. "He needs constant care, you know," he whispered to her in the acrid booming gloom. "The drugs got him over the shock, but he can't tolerate more, and he'll be very weak."

True, she said with feathers rather than voice. Aloud: "Olga shall nurse him. She cannot get around as easily as Rusa or I, and lacks your physical strength. Besides, she can prepare meals and the like for us."

Pete nodded absently. He had a dread to explain. "Uh . . . uh . . . do you think—well, I mean in your ethic, in the New Faith—might Enherrian put an end to himself?" And he wondered if God would really blame the captain.

Her wings and tail spread, her chest erected, she glared. "You say that of him?" she shrilled. Seeing his concern, she eased, even made a *krrr* noise which might answer to a chuckle. "No, no, he has his death-pride. He would never rob God of honor."

After survey and experiment, the decision was to hack a giant cross in the island turf. That growth couldn't be ignited, and what wood was burnable—deadfall—was too scant and stingy of smoke for a beacon.

The party had no spades; the vegetable mat was thick and tough; the toil became brutal. Pete, like Whell and Rusa, would return to camp and topple into sleep. He wouldn't rouse till morning, to gulp his food and stumble off to labor. He grew gaunt, bearded, filthy, numb-brained, sore in every cell.

Thus he did not notice how Olga was waning. Enherrian was mending, somewhat, under her care. She did her jobs, which were comparatively light, and would have been ashamed to complain of headaches, giddiness, diarrhea, and nausea. Doubtless she imagined she suffered merely from reaction to disaster, plus a sketchy and ill-balanced diet, plus heat and brilliant sun and—she'd cope.

The days were too short for work, the nights too short for sleep. Pete's terror was that he would see a flitter pass and vanish over the horizon before the Ythrians could hail it. Then they might try sending

Rusa for help. But that was a long, tricky flight; and the gulf coast camp was due to be struck soon.

Sometimes he wondered dimly how he and Olga might do if marooned on Gray. He kept enough wits to dismiss that fantasy for what it was. Take the simple fact that native life appeared to lack certain vitamins—

Then one darkness, perhaps a terrestrial week after the shipwreck, he was aroused by her crying his name. He struggled to wakefulness. She lay beside him. Gray's moon was up, nearly full, swifter and brighter than Luna. Its glow drowned most of the stars, frosted the encroaching bushes, fell without pity to show him her fallen cheeks and rolling eyes. She shuddered in his arms; he heard her teeth clapping. "I'm cold, darling, I'm cold," she said in the subtropical summer night. She vomited over him, and presently she was delirious.

The Ythrians gave what help they could, he what medicines he could. By sunrise (an outrageousness of rose and gold and silver-blue, crossed by the jubilant wings of waterfowl) he knew she was dying.

He examined his own physical state, using a robot he discovered he had in his skull: yes, his wretchedness was due to more than overwork, he saw that now; he too had had the upset stomach and the occasional shivers, nothing like the disintegration which possessed Olga, nevertheless the same kind of thing. Yet the Ythrians stayed healthy. Did a local germ attack humans while finding the other race undevourable?

The rescuers, who came on the island two Gray days later, already had the answer. That genus of bushes is widespread on the planet. A party elsewhere, after getting sick and getting into safety suits, analyzed its vapors. They are a cumulative poison to man; they scarcely harm an Ythrian. The analysts named it the hell shrub.

Unfortunately, their report wasn't broadcast until after the boat left. Meanwhile Pete had been out in the field every day, while Olga spent her whole time in the hollow, over which the sun regularly created an inversion layer.

Whell and Rusa went grimly back to work. Pete had to get away. He wasn't sure of the reason, but he had to be alone when he screamed at heaven, "Why did You do this to her, why did You do it?" Enherrian could look after Olga, who had brought him back to a life he no longer wanted. Pete had stopped her babblings, writhings, and saw-toothed sounds of pain with a shot. She ought to sleep peacefully into that death which the monitor instruments said was, in the absence of hospital facilities, ineluctable.

He stumbled off to the heights. The sea reached calm, in a thousand hues of azure and green, around the living island, beneath the gentle sky. He knelt in all that emptiness and put his question.

After an hour he could say, "Your will be done," and return to camp.

Olga lay awake. "Pete, Pete!" she cried. Anguish distorted her voice till he couldn't recognize it; nor could he really see her in the yellowed sweating skin and lank hair drawn over a skeleton, or find her in the stench and the nails which flayed him as they clutched. "Where were you, hold me close, it hurts, how it hurts—"

He gave her a second injection, to small effect.

He knelt again, beside her. He has not told me what he said, or how. At last she grew quiet, gripped him hard, and waited for the pain to end.

When she died, he said, it was like seeing a light blown out.

He laid her down, closed eyes and jaw, folded her hands. On mechanical feet he went to the pup tent which had been rigged for Enherrian. The cripple calmly awaited him. "She is fallen?" he asked.

Pete nodded.

"That is well," Enherrian said.

"It is not," Pete heard himself reply, harsh and remote. "She shouldn't have aroused. The drug should've—Did you give her a stim shot? Did you bring her back to suffer?"

"What else?" said Enherrian, though he was unarmed and a blaster lay nearby for Pete to seize. *Not that I'll ease him out of his fate!* went through the man in a spasm. "I saw that you, distraught, had misgauged. You were gone and I unable to follow you. She might well die before your return."

Out of his void, Pete gaped into those eyes. "You mean," rattled from him, "You mean . . . she . . . mustn't?"

Enherrian crawled forth—he could only crawl, on his single wing —to take Pete's hands. "My friend," he said, his tone immeasurably compassionate, "I honored you both too much to deny her her death-pride."

Pete's chief awareness was of the cool sharp talons.

"Have I misunderstood?" asked Enherrian anxiously. "Did you not wish her to give God a battle?"

Even on Lucifer, the nights finally end. Dawn blazed on the tors when Pete finished his story.

I emptied the last few cc. into our glasses. We'd get no work done today. "Yeah," I said. "Cross-cultural semantics. Given the best will in the universe, two beings from different planets—or just different countries, often—take for granted they think alike; and the outcome can be tragic."

"I assumed that at first," Pete said. "I didn't need to forgive Enherrian—how could he know? For his part, he was puzzled when I buried my darling. On Ythri they cast them from a great height into wilderness. But neither race wants to watch the rotting of what was loved, and so he did his lame best to help me."

He drank, looked as near the cruel bluish sun as he was able, and mumbled, "What I couldn't do was forgive God."

"The problem of evil," I said.

"Oh, no. I've studied these matters, these past years: read theology, argued with priests, the whole route. Why does God, if He is a loving and personal God, allow evil? Well, there's a perfectly good Christian answer to that. Man—intelligence everywhere—must have free will. Otherwise we're puppets and have no reason to exist. Free will necessarily includes the capability of doing wrong. We're here, in this cosmos during our lives, to learn how to be good of our unforced choice."

"I spoke illiterately," I apologized. "All that brandy. No, sure, your logic is right, regardless of whether I accept your premises or not. What I meant was: the problem of pain. Why does a merciful God permit undeserved agony? If He's omnipotent, He isn't compelled to.

"I'm not talking about the sensation which warns you to take your hand from the fire, anything useful like that. No, the random accident which wipes out a life . . . or a mind—" I drank. "What happened to Arrach, yes, and to Enherrian, and Olga, and you, and Whell. What happens when a disease hits, or those catastrophes we label acts of God. Or the slow decay of us if we grow very old. Every such horror. Never mind if science has licked some of them; we have enough left, and then there were our ancestors who endured them all.

"Why? What possible purpose is served? It's not adequate to declare we'll receive an unbounded reward after we die, and therefore it makes no difference whether a life was gusty or grisly. That's no explanation.

"Is this the problem you're grappling, Pete?"

"In a way." He nodded, cautiously, as if he were already his father's age. "At least, it's the start of the problem.

"You see, there I was, isolated among Ythrians. My fellow humans sympathized, but they had nothing to say that I didn't know already. The New Faith, however. . . . Mind you, I wasn't about to convert. What I did hope for was an insight, a freshness, that'd help me make Christian sense of our losses. Enherrian was so sure, so learned, in his beliefs—

"We talked, and talked, and talked, while I was regaining my strength. He was as caught as I. Not that he couldn't fit our troubles into his scheme of things. That was easy. But it turned out that the New Faith has no satisfactory answer to the problem of *evil*. It says God allows wickedness so that we may win honor by fighting for the right. Really, when you stop to think, that's weak, especially in carnivore Ythrian terms. Don't you agree?"

"You know them, I don't," I sighed. "You imply they have a better answer to the riddle of pain than your own religion does."

"It seems better." Desperation edged his slightly blurred tone:

"They're hunters, or were until lately. They see God like that, as the Hunter. Not the Torturer—you absolutely must understand this point—no, He rejoices in our happiness that way we might rejoice to see a game animal gamboling. Yet at last He comes after us. Our noblest moment is when we, knowing He is irresistible, give Him a good chase, give Him a good fight.

"Then He wins honor. And some infinite end is furthered. (The same one as when my God is given praise? How can I tell?) We're dead, struck down, lingering at most a few years in the memories of those who escaped this time. And that's what we're here for. That's why God created the universe."

"And this belief is old," I said. "It doesn't belong just to a few cranks. No, it's been held for centuries by millions of sensitive, intelligent, educated beings. You can live by it, you can die by it. If it doesn't solve every paradox, it solves some that your faith won't, quite. This is your dilemma, true?"

He nodded again. "The priests have told me to deny a false creed and to acknowledge a mystery. Neither instruction feels right. Or am I asking too much?"

"I'm sorry, Pete," I said, altogether honestly. It hurt. "But how should I know? I looked into the abyss once, and saw nothing, and haven't looked since. You keep looking. Which of us is the braver?

"Maybe you can find a text in Job. I don't know, I tell you, I don't know."

The sun lifted higher above the burning horizon.

the wolfram hunters

BY EDWARD D HOCH

Now in the ninth decade after the Bomb, when the war which had ravaged the earth was almost forgotten, there lived in the upper valley of the Rio Grande a tribe of Indians that had once—in more glorious days—been Apaches. It was not a large tribe, and in the little village called Del Norte there were perhaps no more than two hundred souls.

One of these was the child Running, who passed his days playing and climbing among the foothills much as children everywhere had done in the old days. If there was any difference between Running and these children of the past, it was only that he was alive. Very early in life, certainly before he was seven, Running learned of the old man who lived up on the mountains, a cave-dwelling ogre who easily became the subject of parental threat and childhood legend. "I'll send you to the man on the mountain," parents would say when trying to scare obedience into their offspring. "Be good or the man on the mountain will get you!"

But after he'd passed a certain threshold of age—was it seven or eight or nine?—he realized in a burst of enlightenment that there was nothing to fear from this cave-dwelling creature. The older boys initiated him into the terrors of the cave one stormy night in summer, by the simple expedient of dragging him to its mouth and hurling him inside. The cave in which Running found himself was low and narrow at its entrance, but it soon broadened out into a sort of room where a boy or even a man could stand and walk upright without discomfort.

And the man he found there was far from the horrible bearded ancient he'd come to imagine in his dreams. He was rather a tall and not unhandsome Indian of perhaps forty years, a man who came to greet Running with a smile and an outstretched hand. "You are brave to come here on such a stormy night," he said, and when Running took an uncertain step backward, he added quickly, "Don't be afraid. I am only a man like the others in the valley."

Running summoned all his courage and asked, "Who are you? Why do you live here alone?"

"My name is Legion," he said quietly. "Father Legion. I am a priest, and that is the reason why I must live here, away from other men."

"A priest?" He had heard them mentioned, vaguely, as something that had vanished with the cities and the airplanes and the sea and the rest of it. Vanished with the bursting of the Bombs. "I didn't know there were any left," he told the man.

"I believe I am the only one. At least I am the only one at Del Norte, little friend. But tell me, what is your name?"

"Running."

"Running? I like that name. It is a good name, swift and powerful. What do you know of the far world, little Running? What do you know of the past?"

"Only what they tell me in the councils," Running said, a bit uncertainly. "I am still too young to be initiated into all the mysteries."

The priest smiled at Running as a father would, and said, "Let me tell you about our people, and about the great war that killed so many. Let me tell you why we alone have survived, and how the unfortunate ignorance of a few is perhaps dooming us all to eventual oblivion."

The words, some of them, were strange to the ears of Running, accustomed as he was only to the half-grunted monosyllables of the tribe. But the voice of the priest was gentle, and there was meaning to what he said. Running did not learn it all on the first visit, or the second, but during the months that followed he came again and again to the cave in the hills, and gradually the story of their civilization took shape in his ear and mind and memory.

"Nearly a hundred years ago," Father Legion told him, "men lived in big cities, and flew planes through the air and even ventured as far as the moon you see in the heavens. There were good men and bad men, and sometimes it was difficult to tell which was which. Anyway, presently there came a great war, and rockets fell from the skies all over the world. These rockets, and their Bombs, released something called radiation. It killed people, all people, sometimes at once and sometimes weeks or months later. And here in America everyone died . . . everyone but the Indians."

"But why did we alone live?" Running asked. *Why*, the eternal question.

"We don't exactly know that answer," Father Legion explained, "but of course it must have had something to do with the pigment in our skin. It acted as a natural barrier to the radiation that killed the white man. The other races of the world—the Negro, the Oriental—were not so fortunate. They died too, and only the brown men—that odd mixture of all the races—remained. I suppose in a way it was destined by some greater Power, for now the country which had been our God-given homeland was returned to us."

"But why don't we go to live in the cities?" Running asked one day during their conversation.

"Because, little one, the cities are mostly in ruins. And where buildings remain, the radiation may still be too high even for the Indian to survive. We do not have the intricate measuring devices necessary to be certain of safety. We know only that we have been safe for three generations here at Del Norte, and so we remain here."

"But what about you? Why do you live up here?"

"After the Bomb, a great many people gave up any consolation that religion might have offered them. In those final days of blind fury, churches were burned and priests were slaughtered in the streets, and truly it seemed to the survivors as if the end of the world had finally come to pass. But as I said, the Indians survived. Rather than being thankful to God for the survival, they reflected the sins of the white man. The few Indian priests were not killed, but they were driven into the hills." He paused a moment, as if seeing it all once more on some giant screen before his eyes. "And so we have lived out our years in places like this, worshipping God and searching out others—boys like yourself—to take our place when the time comes."

"I don't want to," Running said quickly, suddenly feeling a bolt of fear through his young body. "I don't want to be like you and live in this cave all my life!"

"Come, come. I'm not asking you to, am I? A boy like you was born to run and play and enjoy life too much to be content up here. I am only telling you a story, because this is something all of you should know."

"Why don't you come down and tell the others, then?" Running asked, playing absently with a stone that was smooth and cool to his touch.

"Because they will not have me. They let me live, probably because their superstitious natures kept them from killing me—or those who came before me. They let me live, if only to serve as a frightening example to bad children. And instead of rebuilding a lost civilization, they spend their days in search of wolfram."

Running knew of the quest for the precious metal, a quest which was carried out only by the warriors of the tribe. Each day they went off into the hills, never wandering too far from the valley, but searching, ever searching for the dark stones of their strange destiny. "Why do they search?" Running asked.

"Because wolfram is the source of the metal tungsten, and in their half-memories of the world as it was, they connect it with electricity and electric lights."

"Electric lights?"

Father Legion nodded. "Once whole cities glowed with light, my son, and it was the light of a million candles. But the light had to be generated. There is no magic in the metal wolfram that will bring it back." And he shook his head sadly, adding half to himself, "Such a long way to fall in only ninety years."

Finally, the annual feast of Easter drew near, and Running was as busy as the others with the preparations for it. The tribal leader, Volyon, was everywhere at once, instructing, ordering, planning. The year's precious gathering of wolfram had to be collected and treated for the ceremonies. And most important of all the prisoners must be anointed and prepared for execution. It was this last part of the annual ceremonies which drew from Father Legion the greatest condemnation, and Running had never seen him as angry as the afternoon they talked of it.

"A blasphemous, profane thing!" the priest told him. "To crucify these men in the manner of Christ!"

"They are criminals," Running argued, because he could see nothing wrong in the annual custom which never failed to provide a few days' excitement.

"Some of them are murderers," Father Legion admitted. "But

more are simply poor men who drank too much or had the wrong friends. To keep them penned up during the whole year and then to put them to death at Easter time—and such a death!"

"Our leader Volyon says it is a religious death," Running replied, but for the first time he wondered if a doubt had crossed his mind. For the few years he could remember well, the annual observance had been the high point of the year. But he had to admit cruelty in the proceedings. Any member of the village of two-hundred-odd who committed a crime during the year was arrested, tried by a council of elders, and imprisoned. Thus a man might spend up to a year in jail before the fatal day of his execution arrived. And the horrible penalty of crucifixion was meted out for a variety of offences ranging from murder and rape to the stealing of wolfram and sleeping on guard duty.

"It is a perversion of religion," Father Legion insisted, and he told Running the story of the Christ, as it had been told by so many through the centuries.

And when he'd finished, Running asked, "You learned all this from the priest ahead of you?"

"And the priest ahead of him," Father Legion said with a little nod. And then, almost to himself, he added, "I suppose I am a bishop really, or perhaps even the Pope, if I am truly the last one left." Then, louder, "How old are you, my son?"

"Nearly ten, I think."

"And you have been coming here since last summer, listening to me talk. Surely a boy your age would rather run and play with the others."

"No, no," Running said, barely believing the words himself. "I would rather be here with you."

And so that evening again Running returned to the settlement in the valley, by the shores of the river, and as before he spoke to no one about his meeting with the priest in the cave, or about the strange and wonderful things he was learning there. His mother and sisters were busy with the Easter preparations, and his father was up in the hills with the wolfram hunters.

On the following day, Running saw that the terrible rite about which Father Legion had spoken was beginning its annual re-enactment on the hill, before his eyes. The prisoners—there were nine of them—were brought before the tribal leader, Volyon. Very carefully he read the sentences, which all of them knew so well already. One man, Crow, was a murderer, and he accepted the death sentence with eyes downcast at the dusty earth. Another, Raincloud, who had stolen another man's allotment of wolfram, cried out to his brothers and relatives as he was led to one of the nine wooden crosses. His mother tried to break through the line of guards, but they held her back.

The rest was a nightmare, clouding the mind of Running, terrifying him as it never had before. Towards the end, when the last of the nine was being lashed to his cross, Running looked away, back toward the little line of frame houses. But even in this vista there was no escaping the sight or sound of it. He saw that final cross reflected in a broken windowpane, saw it distorted by the cracked glass into a shattered image of life, and death. He closed his eyes tightly as the last of the nine screamed out his fright in the face of death, then stopped suddenly in mid-scream as the ceremonial arrows found his naked chest.

Afterward, when the nine condemned men had become simply nine punctured corpses hanging from their crosses on the hilltop, Volyon left the warrior Samely on guard and led the others back down to the village. Still the relatives of the executed men cried and screamed, for the idea of death is difficult to accept, even with many months to prepare for it. These families knew now that their loved ones were dead with bodies fated to hang up there for many days until the sun and the buzzards had done their work, until the lesson had been well learned by those who remained.

But even in a village as small as this, Running knew there would be more men to die next Easter. And perhaps a woman too. There had been a woman last year. He had never known her crime for sure, but the others had spoken of it in whispers. This night he hid in a remote corner of the house and took no part in the rites as he had that previous year. This night he covered his ears against the sounds of Volyon's prayers and the singing of the warrior Mancoat. He heard his father return to the house once for more of the grain spirits they drank on such occasions, but still he did not stir. The hour grew late, and dark and presently quiet. And Running slept.

In the morning the village woke slowly to the cares of a new day. There were more ceremonies, including the offering of the wolfram to Volyon, and his own symbolic offering in turn to heaven, but for Running there was still the memory of the men on the hill. He ran up early to see them, praying perhaps that they would be still alive, or at least finally buried. But the nine crosses still stood in the morning sun, and when he came too close Samely chased him away with a wave of his spear.

Running remembered stories of guns that fired bullets, and for many years after the Bomb the Indians had continued to use such weapons. Now, though, the bullets were gone, used up, and the tribe had reverted to the bow and arrow and the spear. Running had seen a rifle once, dust-covered in his uncle's house, but he had been afraid to touch it.

He played on the hill for a time with the other boys, and they wrestled around, showing off for the guards who took time out from their duties to watch. No one even remembered now what the valley was guarded against, whether the unknown enemy of long ago had been dying white men, or other Indians, or even Mexicans up from the south. The enemy had never come, whoever he was, though someone like Father Legion would have claimed he was already there.

Towards noon Running noticed a disturbance in the village, and as he drew nearer he heard the voice of Mancoat's wife pleading with Volyon. "I have looked everywhere," she said. "My husband has disappeared."

She was a pretty woman named Airing, very popular with the men of the village, and even Running was aware of the care Mancoat always took in watching over her. Now Volyon placed a comforting arm around her shoulders, and said, "I am sure he will turn up, little one. He was with me last night, and his voice was raised to the heavens in song."

"But where *is* he?"

"Perhaps he has gone in search of more wolfram."

But Airing shook her head. "You need not tell me that, Volyon. You well know that no one goes after wolfram during the holidays."

"Anyway, come with me," he said. "We will ask the guards."

Running watched them go off, and then ran down to the house to tell his mother and father and sisters of this strange development. No one had ever disappeared from the village before. Where was there to disappear?

By nightfall the village was in an uproar. Volyon personally had led a search of all the houses when the guards had reported no one leaving the area, but no trace of the missing man had been found. Running was standing nearby when he heard one of the ancient warriors, Treetop, say to Volyon, "What about the priest's cave? That has not been searched."

Volyon nodded and raised his spear high in the air, motioning for the search group to follow. They made their way along the hillside until at last they reached the half-hidden little cave, and Running followed in the darkness unnoticed.

Father Legion had heard their approach, and now he appeared in the entrance, holding high his torch. The flickering flamelight played on the faces of those who had gathered around him. "What is it you want?" he asked coldly.

Treetop started to speak, but Volyon signalled him to silence. "Oh, priest, we come in search of Mancoat who has disappeared. His wife Airing is greatly worried."

Father Legion stared hard at Volyon. "You may search my home if you wish," he said.

While the others searched, old Treetop drew close and said, "I remember you as a boy. I will always remember you as a boy."

The priest nodded. "This is something I have to do," he said. "You wouldn't understand."

"Neither would your mother," the old warrior said, turning away.

They searched the cave carefully, but found no evidence that Mancoat had been there. Finally, discouraged, they filed back down the hillside. But Running remained with the priest for a time, and asked him, "Who is Treetop, Father Legion? He knows you from long ago."

"He was very close to me at one time," the priest answered. "He was my father."

And after a time Running followed the others down the hill, because there didn't seem to be any more to say.

In the morning, he was surprised to see Father Legion coming down the hill to the village accompanied by one of the stately guards. He had never seen the priest in the village before and he feared what this might mean. But Father Legion went directly to the house of Volyon, which was the largest in the valley. When Running saw that the tribal leader was not at home, he ran quickly to the side of the priest, feeling the stones sharp and smooth beneath his hardened feet.

"Father Legion, I think he still searches for the missing Mancoat."

"Thank you, Running," the priest said, brushing the hair on the boy's head with a kindly hand. "I came to see him about that matter."

"You saw the men they executed, Father Legion?"

The priest glanced up at the far hill, where nine crosses still stood outlined in the first rays of morning-light. "Yes," he said quietly. "I saw them."

From somewhere Mancoat's wife Airing appeared, still close to tears. There seemed no way to comfort her, short of finding her missing husband. "Where is Volyon?" she asked.

"I seek him myself," the priest told her.

"I . . . I fear that Mancoat is dead. I have this awful feeling that someone has murdered him. The men of the village, they look at me so oddly. It is a look one reserves for widows."

"Who looked at you that way?"

"Many people. One was the brother of Raincloud, who hangs up there." She motioned towards the hill without looking. "Could someone have killed Mancoat and thrown him into the river?"

Their eyes sought the water at her words, but the stream ran shallow for the springtime. "No," Father Legion said softly, "but perhaps . . ."

At that moment, Volyon came, followed closely by old Treetop and some others. "The priest!" Volyon exclaimed, startled. Treetop looked away.

"I have come to talk of many things," Father Legion said.

Volyon nodded. "We can talk here, on my porch. The sun is good today."

"Have you found Mancoat?" his wife asked.

"No . . . not yet."

"He's dead! I know he's dead!"

Volyon motioned to old Treetop, who placed a gnarled hand of comfort on the girl. Father Legion took the opportunity to motion Running to one side. "Young Running, could you do me a great favour?"

"Anything, Father Legion."

"You see that man pausing for bath water from the river?"

"Karlong, brother of the dead Raincloud."

"Correct. Follow him for me, and report to me where he goes."

"But . . ."

"No questions now, little one. Be quick!"

Then he turned back to Volyon and the others, and Running had to hurry on to his mission. The tall Karlong, a great beast of a man, had already rounded the corner of a house with his burden of bath water, but oddly enough he seemed headed away from the village proper. Running tried to follow in a casual manner, skipping as if in play through occasional sections of tall grass. But the big man was on his guard. He looked back constantly, frowning once when he caught sight of Running.

Soon, though, he reached his destination, a section of flatland hidden from the view of the village. It was a desolate area where Running had only rarely ventured, even in play. Here even the trees seemed dead, for this was the village's burial ground.

And as Karlong poured his carefully carried water upon the grass in one particular area, Running suddenly realized the truth—what better place to hide a body than in a burial ground? Karlong had killed Mancoat and hidden his body here, and now he was watering the grass upon the grave.

Then Karlong saw him.

He turned to run, but the big man was fast in pursuit. He could almost feel the hot breath of doom on his back as he ran higher, even higher up the hill. If only he could reach one of the guard positions before Karlong caught him. If only . . .

He had not been named Running for nothing. His feet were swift and his legs worked hard, reminding him of the pictures of pistons he'd seen once in a book at Volyon's great library. Karlong still followed, panting, but now the gap between them had widened and Running knew he would not be caught. Over the next hill and he would be safe for sure. He topped it and saw Samely standing guard near the nine crosses with their burdens. He paused for breath and looked behind him. Karlong had given up the chase and was heading back towards the village.

"What are you doing, boy?" Samely called out to him.

"Only playing." Running stooped and gathered a few pebbles in his hand, and went hopping off down the hill, in pretended search for some unlucky rabbit or gopher.

Back at Volyon's house, he saw that Father Legion was still conferring with their leader. The two sat close together, like old friends, but even Running could see that their conversation was anything but friendly. He crept closer to listen.

"You want us to backtrack, return to the white man's way of life?" Volyon was saying. "He lived in his great cities while the Indian nearly starved on reservations. He treated us like cattle, something to be herded here and there, to be settled in one spot until the government needed the land for a new highway or a power project, then shunted off once more to some new and more crowded life elsewhere. You want us to build towards that sort of life again?"

"But with an Indian civilization, how could it happen?" Father Legion asked, his voice still calm.

"With an Indian civilization we would only find someone else to dominate. Perhaps we would find some lost group of Mexicans whom we could force from their land."

Father Legion stirred in his chair. "You are a wise man, Volyon. Wiser than I had thought. You realize that the sins you mention are the sins of civilization rather than the sins of the white man alone."

Volyon's temper cooled. "We both know much of the past, Father Legion. You were wise even as a child, and I can understand in a way your decision to join Father Blaming up on the hill. He was a good man too. I am sorry he is dead."

"You could at least give me a chance to live down here again, back among your people and mine."

"As a priest?"

"Of course."

"It would only end in bloodshed."

"I don't think so."

"What could you give them that they don't already have? Besides your white man's civilization?"

". . . A knowledge of God."

"And what would that do for them?"

"It might prevent things like this," Father Legion said, gesturing towards the distant hill.

"Do you want to prevent that? Do you want those men running loose to rob and kill again?"

"Is this sort of punishment any determent? To leave them hanging there until their bodies rot in the sun, or are eaten by the buzzards?"

"You ask if it is a deterring factor and I answer you. Last Easter there were eleven bodies hanging there, and the year before that there were fifteen."

"Can we afford the loss of such a percentage of our population?" Father Legion asked.

Volyon shrugged. "Crime must be punished. By my methods, not by yours."

"The man who vanished—Mancoat—has not been found? Suppose I locate him for you."

"We have searched the entire village and the hills. As you well know. If we could not find him, how will you be able to?" "*If* I find him," the priest persisted, "would you agree to let me live in peace in the village? And instruct the people?"

Volyon was silent for a long time. He seemed to be staring off towards the distant hills, considering his answer. "Very well," he said finally. "If you find Mancoat, you can return to the village in peace. But I warn you that the people will never listen."

"All I ask is a chance to speak to them. The civilization I spoke of will not come overnight, but a start must be made."

"You really think it will be better this time? Better than before the Bomb?"

Father Legion looked down at the rough wooden floor. "It has to be, or God wouldn't have saved the few of us. He's given us another chance, you see."

Volyon sighed. "Very well." He got to his feet and looked up at the sky, studying the changing, gathering clouds. "Now where is the missing Mancoat? His wife is anxious."

The priest's eyes clouded. "I can only offer the solace of prayer to Airing. Her husband is dead. Murdered."

"Murdered!"

And Father Legion reached over the porch to grasp at Running. "Come out, little one. I see you lurking there."

"I . . . I only just got back, Father Legion."

"And where did the mighty Karlong lead you?"

"Karlong!" Volyon gasped out. "Did he . . . ?"

"Where, little one?"

"To the graveyard. He was watering a freshly turned plot of earth."

"The graveyard!" Volyon gasped. "Come, quickly!"

They followed him, already caught up in the sense of nameless haste, now nearly running over the vague grasslands, splashing through wandering streams that drifted lazily towards the growing river. Others were coming, sensing the excitement, and Running saw Airing and old Treetop in the lead. Soon the graveyard appeared before them, calm and peaceful in the springtime sun.

"Karlong!" the leader shouted. "Come out of there, Karlong!"

The big man rose slowly from behind a tombstone, holding a short spear ready in his hand. "Keep back," he said softly.

And Father Legion stepped around Volyon, walking deliberately into the range of the spear. "Put it down, Karlong," he said. "We know everything."

"Keep back!"

"We know about the body in that fresh grave. Put down your spear."

The big man moved, but not as fast as the priest. Father Legion hurled himself through the distance between them, carrying Karlong backwards over a tombstone. In a moment the others were upon him. They pulled him gasping, weaponless, to his feet, and Volyon faced him with all the splendour of a chieftain. "Dog!" he spat out through curled lips. "You have murdered a fellow human being!"

But now Father Legion broke through, brushing the grass from his body. "No, no," he insisted, "you don't understand. None of you understand. He didn't murder Mancoat. His only crime was in burying his brother, and who among you can call that a crime?"

"His brother!"

Father Legion nodded. "The body in the grave is that of Raincloud, whom you executed two days ago."

"But that is impossible," old Treetop said, still clutching the young girl in his arms. "Raincloud still hangs on his cross upon the hill."

"Does he?" the priest questioned. "Let us go up and see. But you might keep Airing here. It will not be a pleasant sight for her."

They mounted the hillside in silence, each man with his own thoughts, and they made their way uncertainly to the second cross in the line of nine. Upon it, his face twisted in a final grimace of pain, hung the missing Mancoat.

Father Legion looked up at him once, then turned away sadly as others cut down the body. "But who would do such a thing?" Volyon asked.

The priest closed his eyes against the glare of the sun. "Sleeping on guard duty is punishable by the death penalty," he said. "When Samely awoke that first night and saw that the second cross was empty, he had to do something. I imagine Mancoat happened by about that time, and Samely killed him. Killed him and hung his body in the place of Raincloud."

"There he goes!" someone shouted, and they turned as one man to see the guard Samely running down the hill. They were after him in an instant, and the hunters who went daily for the wolfram in the hills now ran him quickly to earth, and their knives flashed in a vengeance that would not need another Easter's judgment.

Father Legion put a damp hand to his forehead. "God grant that he be the last one to die here by violence."

"How did you know, Father Legion?" Volyon asked, and Running moved closer to hear the priest's answer.

"I am not a detective, or even a wise man. After Raincloud's brother removed him from the cross, Samely needed only another body to fill the space. None of you, he knew, would look closely at nine corpses rotting in the sun. And by burial time, who could tell the difference? But last night I did look closely at those nine corpses. I mounted the hill to say the prayer for the dead under each man, and I saw Mancoat hanging there. I also saw Samely dozing under a tree."

Volyon cleared his throat. "There will be no more such executions, Father Legion. I have at least learned that lesson. And, I think, no more guards to risk death by sleeping on duty."

"That will be a start," the priest said. And he turned to Running. "Come, my son, we have a world to win. . . ."

the gift of nothing

BY JOAN C. HOLLY

Martin Sunbear scrambled to his feet at the sound of crackling underbrush. Birds shrieked as shouts broke the green Kana silence. It was Hayden's voice, loud and out of breath. Martin leaped the brook that curled through the glen, and ran to meet the voice.

The bushes parted and Tiva ran toward him, her tanned arms outstretched, cradling a small animal. The same sun that made highlights in her black hair glinted in the tears on her cheeks. She stopped, looking at Martin with her black eyes unbelieving.

Hayden, the crew's medic, came behind her, blond and red-faced, his mouth open to shout, but Martin motioned him down. As Alien Contact Officer for the *Wasp*, he had the right of way in emergencies with Kana's natives, and from the distress of the girl's face, this was an emergency. He glanced at the animal. It was brown and soft-furred, the closest thing to a rabbit Kana spawned. Its head and feet hung limply over Tiva's arm. It was dead.

"He killed it," Tiva whispered. "It was running, and he killed it."

They were simple words. Simple enough for Martin to understand without the Translator hookup to the ship's language computer. But he would have known, anyway, from the hurt in her voice and the charred hole in the animal.

Hayden couldn't hold back any longer. "What the hell, it's just a rabbit. She wouldn't listen to reason. She picked it up and started running."

"Did you touch *her?*" Martin demanded.

"No! I followed the prissy rules."

Martin took the animal and laid it gently on the grass. Then he stood staring at it because he didn't know what else to do. Finally he said, "Get a Translator hookup, Hayden. I may need it."

"Why?" Hayden bridled. "It's just a rabbit. It's not that important. Just a woman's idea of pity. You don't need a hookup, anyway. You're fluent."

Martin bit his lip and agreed. Tuned to the language-computer on the *Wasp*, the speaker-transmitter hookup helped whenever a conversation demanded more fluency than any of the crew possessed. But he seldom needed it anymore. He had "taught" the computer at first and then learned from it as fast as it could extrapolate. He was fluent. The other crew members rarely bothered to study the alien language out of their own laziness and their confidence that he would do it.

With communication easier they had all thought their job would be a snap, but something had been wrong about this planet from the start. Since the *Wasp* had first set down two months ago and radioed her safe landing to the mother-ship, *Astra*, Martin had felt a queerness in his stomach. But he could never catch it close enough to examine. More than anything else, it felt like nostalgia—like homesickness—and that was ridiculous.

Meeting the natives and being accepted was almost too easy. The people of Kana were gentle people—kind, happy, and religious. They wore flowers and feathers in their hair and laughed a lot. Brandon, captain of the *Wasp*, called them children. Martin didn't know. They lived as a Stage Four culture should live—in villages of about fifty families, in shelters made of natural materials, with primitive utensils and primitive ceremonies. Beneath their feet were gold, uranium, oil and iron. Around them was an Eden-like world of rich land, clear water and tall forests. There were no carnivores, and the Kanans were vegetarians. They knew life's worth and were contented. But they were unaware that with the descent of the *Wasp*, their world had changed, and they might lose their future.

Tiva stood beside him now, her dark eyes pitiful. He asked her without the hookup, "Tell me what happened, Tiva—please. What made you cry?"

She pointed to the dead animal. "He killed it. I tried to stop him, but he killed it. How could he do that? How could he stand it?"

Hayden shrugged away in disgust, understanding only a bit of what was said.

Martin probed gently, "You are crying for the animal?" He hoped

that was all it was. Seeing Hayden running behind her had given him
a start. Tiva was too pretty, and there had been one "incident" already.

But she nodded, "Yes. For its spirit. For its freedom and its life.
He killed it."

"Is she going to make a big thing out of this?" Hayden fumed.
"Can't you make her see it's only a rabbit?"

Tiva turned on him, responding to his tone of voice even though
she didn't understand his actual words. She demanded in her own
language, "You took this life. What right did you have? Can you make
it walk again?"

Hayden swiveled away from her accusing eyes. "What's she talking about, Sunbear?"

"She's trying to tell you what I've said all along. These people
don't think anyone has the right to kill. In other words, it's the fifth
commandment taken seriously; Thou shalt not kill—period. No specifi-
cations. Just, Thou shalt not kill. You knew better."

"I didn't think you meant rabbits."

"I meant *insects,*" Martin answered, then sighed, "You go back
to the *Wasp* and leave us alone. I'll try to make her understand."

Hayden left without argument, and Martin began the task of
making Tiva see that different people have different values; that, to
Hayden, an animal was not equal in life. He had to repeat and repeat
to dispel the disbelief on her face. And somehow, telling her made him
a little sick. It went against something he'd thought he buried long ago
—an inherited resentment that had no place in the modern age.

But he had to make her forgive the mistake. As the daughter of
Chantuka, principal chief of Kana, her feelings carried weight. The old
man was walking the edge, swaying between accepting or rejecting their
treaty. She could push him to the "no" side.

So he stood in the glade and talked hesitantly in a language that
was still only half-learned until he saw her waver and heard her forgive.
As an Alien Contact Officer, he knew his trade. But this was the first
time he had felt it to be a trade of traitors.

The fire glowed with yellow cracklings and sent shadows jumping
into the night and onto the faces of the people circled around it. Two
of the four crewmen, Hayden and Lyler, were on one side of the circle

with some young native men, and Martin sat on Chantuka's left, Captain Brandon beside him and the missionary, Mr. Evers, next to Brandon. Martin's sole duty was to translate what Brandon was telling the chief about the benefits of a treaty with the other worlds in his attempt to convince the old man to agree to it.

Evers was saying nothing on this particular night. He'd had his innings against Chantuka's god off and on for two months. Tonight he simply listened, his thin, gentle face interested, but calm.

Brandon was a different matter. He was intent and anxious as he filled the old man's head full of the wonders the Kanans would receive in return for permission to establish colonial and mining settlements, listing gifts of plows and tractors for their agricultural economy, medicines, and new knowledge that would boost them overnight from primitive to civilized.

Chantuka remained dignified and quiet, his head tilted toward Martin's translations only slightly, as though the sound was not welcome, just inevitable. He listened and weighed, but never answered.

Brandon tried a new approach, bringing things down to examples so Chantuka could understand. The big, brown-haired, immaculate captain creased his brow and pretended he was talking to a child.

"You've seen our flying machine, Chantuka," he said. "We need materials to feed that machine and all the others like it. Those things you have, underground, deep in your world. If you give permission, my people will come here and dig for them, and in return for your kindness, we will pay you in fine new gifts. Your people will have a new life opened to them. They can be rich and proud. The settlers will come, too, and you'll have new friends, new teachers, new brothers."

As Martin translated, Chantuka remained silent. Only the deepening of his wrinkles showed that he had heard. The firelight glistened in his white hair, and Martin thought there was nothing stern in his face. His life had been too simple for that. Instead, there was wisdom. But Brandon couldn't see it.

Martin was comfortable near Chantuka. The nostalgia disappeared in the chief's presence and he felt at home. But that, too, was ridiculous.

He had never really had a home. He had never belonged anywhere. Somehow the culture of his civilization hadn't gotten through to him. He knew the rules and followed them, but there was some tremendous ingredient lacking. Other people were happy and fulfilled. He was not. He had no roots—no rapport with any of it.

Sometimes when he was on Earth and could attend a monthly chapter meeting of the United Indian Nation, and sit with his own kind in the dim light of a lodgefire and listen to the drums beating rhythms that echoed in the heart and the blood—sometimes, then, he felt at home. But those meetings were few, and when they ended it always meant returning to the bright light of the city waiting outside, watching the feathers being put carefully away and the proper modern street dress slipped back on bodies that for a few hours had been transported backwards in time to another age, another culture.

He often hated the UIN meetings simply because they had to end. Yet he was grateful that his people had managed to increase themselves, take their place in the predominant society so that they could live, and then in a great needing-of-each-other, create and give life to the UIN that preserved the best things from their old ways. Their Indian heritage was strong in all of them and not to be given up, although it made them still suspect among the rest of society, still open to prejudice here and there.

But many times he'd thought that the heritage wasn't as strong in most as it was in himself. The others left the UIN meetings with a quicker step than he, more willing to reenter the outside world, and their attitude only heightened his own resentment. The old ways could never really "be" again, but he had to consciously force himself to accept that fact.

He had wondered if he belonged somewhere else—if there might be a place where he could find the fulfillment other people found— perhaps on some other world. But the search among the stars hadn't provided that place. He was a man between. And the necessary study of history and myriad cultures in order to become an Alien Contact Officer had only deepened his loneliness.

Yet, Kana had an odd effect on him. The Kanans were strangely familiar, not only in their echoing of the copper-bronze of his skin and the black of his hair. It was more. They touched the same spirit in him that the old, lost culture stirred to life. But if Kana turned out to be "his" place in the universe, how could he keep it? With the coming of missionaries, miners, and colonizers, Kana would become one more link in the chain of Earth's society. And then the door would close and he would again have no home. Here, by Chantuka, he could at least pretend for a while.

But Brandon continued to rupture the mood. He switched to English entirely and spoke gruffly. "You're not giving me much help, Sunbear. These people are tame enough. Why won't they come through?"

"Maybe they're too tame," Martin answered, not sure, himself, what he really meant. "Anyway, persuading them isn't my job."

"But I get the feeling you're pulling the other way. I think the old man senses it, too. He likes you, and he'll trust your judgment." Brandon leaned closer. "We've got to have this planet. It's the richest strike in years. Land—ore—forests—. Lyler's got his first mineral estimates finished and he says it's fantastic. There shouldn't be any problem. We've made treaties with people worse than cannibals. Where's the trouble?"

Martin shifted, reluctant to answer. "I think it's a matter of philosophy. Religion, if you like. These people aren't cannibals. They're not like any people we've met. They're an old, old race."

"And pagan," said Evers, the expedition's missionary.

Martin glanced at him, keeping his face expressionless. He couldn't argue with Evers. The missionary was a man with decent intentions. One missionary accompanied each scouting trip to begin the conversion of the people to Standard Christianity—the Standard Faith —and to protect the natives, when possible, from the harsher realities of alien contact. At least that was what they "thought" they were doing. Martin often had his own ideas.

Brandon said, "They haven't progressed one iota in who knows how many years. They're stuck in some backward time slot."

"They're happy," Martin answered. "Why should they change?"

"Happy, perhaps," Evers inserted his voice again, "but certainly not striving toward the proper morality, not obeying the only true God. I have to agree with Captain Brandon. They're caught in a backward time slot. I'm not really interested in the crusade for a treaty, Martin. You know that. I only want to bring these people into God's fold."

Martin read the sincerity on the man's face. But Evers, too, didn't look beyond his personal view to the result of what he wanted to do on Kana. He and Brandon were working from different starting points, but heading for the same locus—colonization, change, and to Martin's mind —ruin. He wasn't even certain why he felt the coming ruin so strongly in the pit of his stomach. He had helped to make treaties with other worlds and had never sensed this reluctance in himself before.

"They need us," Brandon insisted. "Look what we can do for them." Martin could almost taste the captain's frustration. Brandon believed that no one could be truly happy without the things that made *him* happy. He had things in his hands to give the Kanans, but Chantuka refused to accept them. "What I need is something tangible I can use to prove my point. Something dramatic, maybe. Think about it, Sunbear. We don't have much time. The *Astra* will be leaving this system in three weeks and I have to take this planet back with me. Peacefully."

"All I can give you is a word of warning," Martin scowled across the circle where Hayden and Lyler were teaching some young men to shoot craps. "Keep the crew in line. Don't let another incident occur. And stop treating Chantuka like a child. Be careful what you say because he believes every word. He doesn't know about stretching the truth."

Brandon stared at him hard, trying to see the emotion behind his words. Brandon had sensed that something about him didn't ring true anymore. "Your feathers starting to show, Sunbear? You think only savages can be honest?"

Martin let the snide remark pass as he always did. Bigotry, it seemed, had an eternal life of its own.

When he got no response to his baited stab, Brandon straightened and made his tone official. "Three more weeks is all the time we have. When that's up, we've got to have a treaty."

Martin tightened his jaw. He understood. Men in the Scouting Service never failed because the alternative was too grave for both sides. When a suitable planet was found, it was taken, "suitable" meaning only that it was habitable and held no biological danger. Biological quarantine was the *only* exception. If the planet wasn't raped by treaty, it was raped by force, and when it came to violence, both natives and invaders died.

Chantuka would decide it all for Kana, and as much as he ached to, Martin wasn't allowed to tell him that his choice was really between agreement or invasion.

Evers cleared his throat and offered, "Perhaps if I keep trying, captain. Let me go on talking to Chantuka about God and the new Path that I can teach his people. He listens when I talk. I may be able to persuade him to your treaty by making him want religion."

"*Our* religion," Martin muttered. "Our hodgepodge."

"What does hodgepodge mean?" Evers challenged him. His eyes were sharper now, his gentleness less apparent.

"Forget it," Martin said, then reversed himself and spoke his mind. "What else can you call taking every organized religion that existed on Earth and incorporating them all into one? And then even adding dogma from some other powerful cultures we've met just to get them to go along with us more willingly?"

Evers' voice chilled, "You think I preach hodgepodge? How were you raised, Martin Sunbear? Weren't you instructed in the Standard Faith?"

Martin shrugged. He didn't want to admit another personal difference to set him still further apart. But he wouldn't lie, either. "I was instructed in the Standard Faith. But my parents also taught me Christianity."

"The old, narrow Christianity?"

Martin admitted it. "According to that 'obsolete' book called the Bible. Yes."

Brandon guffawed. "You redskins never could stick to the law, could you? I'll bet that Bible was well laced with chants and spirit dances. Incredible!"

Martin suddenly wanted to confess to that accusation, too; he suddenly wanted to get it all out as he had never done before. He *had* been taught the rudiments of the ancient tribal beliefs, and he had gone further, haunting libraries and studying it for himself. But those facts weren't for Brandon's ears.

He sighed, sure he should have kept his mouth closed in the first place. He was only here as an interpreter tonight. And he had to stem the disagreement before it could turn into an argument because he noticed that Chantuka was leaning closer, gazing steadily at their faces, anxious to understand their conversation even though he only knew a word or two of their language.

"Forgive me for saying anything, Mr. Evers," Martin apologized. "I don't usually interfere."

"No, I guess not!" Brandon said. "You're usually the stoic all the way around. I've always figured you needed watching."

It was a direct challenge, but Martin couldn't take it up. "Please, let's not go on with this because certain parties shouldn't hear us quarrel," he warned. "Tone of voice is as understandable as actual words."

Evers and Brandon followed his glance to Chantuka, realized his meaning, and immediately resumed their former relaxed postures. Evers jumped right back to what he had been telling Brandon before, as though nothing had come between. "I still believe it would be the best course, captain. Let *me* talk to the old man. In my own time. I can convince him that our way is what God wants of him."

Martin thought bitterly to himself, *"Scare* him into believing it, you mean." He didn't voice it.

"All right," Brandon agreed. "Talk. I'll lay off a week on you, preacher, but no more. I can't chance any more than that."

Another week passed as Mr. Evers huddled with Chantuka, pressing into his ears stories of how God was vengeful and angry when people didn't follow His appointed ways once they had learned about Him from the proper source.

Evers was becoming decently proficient in the Kanan language, himself, and with the use of a computer hookup, had little need of Martin, so Martin gratefully left the constant talks, a foul taste in his mouth that came from translating words *he* didn't believe for the benefit of an old and wise native who was *learning* to believe them—or at least to fear that they might be true.

Martin took the days to further his own desires, to study the Kanans closely. He could have called it part of his duty as Alien Contact Officer, but he knew it wasn't, because he learned their customs and mores as he had learned no others on the many worlds he had seen.

Everything was sharing and joy on Kana. Even the work was made easy by singing and games. Morning and night, as the sun rose and fell, the people gathered to face the light, and Chantuka offered prayers to their God. "Greeting the sun," it had been called by Martin's own people; thanking God for the light and life He gave them each day. The serenity on the Kanans' faces reached inside Martin and twisted into a ball, fighting something else that crouched there.

One thing he knew. These people were different. Most of the aliens he had met were counterparts of Earthborn man. They waged their fights for survival on worlds varying in harshness and developed suitable degrees of ruthlessness to exist. They had benefited from contact and found good places in the galaxy.

But the Kanans had not fought their world. They had adapted to it. And Martin had an awful premonition that they would be trampled in the maze of machines and foreign humanity. It was like putting a fawn with a tiger, in the belief that the fawn would benefit.

Yet, in spite of the dread, he had to help win the treaty. The weaponless Kanans would be annihilated in an invasion.

When there were only two days left before the *Wasp* had to return to the *Astra*, Chantuka's wife was conspicuously absent from her place at the dawn ceremony. There was a frown under the dignity of the chief's face, and when he lowered his arms from the final gesture of the prayer, he turned immediately for his lodge and disappeared inside.

For once, Brandon had been observing the ceremony with Martin, and as Chantuka entered his lodge, Brandon followed him to investigate the woman's absence and the strange, new hush that hung over the village. Martin returned to the *Wasp* alone. Although Chantuka had become his friend, he didn't share Brandon's lack of consideration for the chief's privacy and didn't want to intrude on him.

When Brandon finally climbed up the ladder and into the *Wasp* a few minutes later, his face was red with haste and excitement. He kept his voice low as though he were discussing a secret, and since Martin was the only available crewman to talk to, he talked to him. "It's the chief's wife, all right. She's down—but good. Chantuka says she's been in pain all night."

"What's wrong with her?" Martin asked, worried. He liked the old woman, although he had seen little of her. She was just a quiet shadow in his mind, but a gentle, smiling shadow that hovered near Chantuka or her daughter, Tiva, or her son. "We haven't seen any disease all the time we've been here." Hayden, their biologist and medic, hadn't even been able to isolate anything on Kana that looked vaguely deadly.

Brandon frowned and stared him straight in the eye. "I don't like telling you this, and I want you to hold yourself in close check, Sunbear. You were deliberately left out of this decision. Now that it's all worked out, I suppose it's time for you to know. I said I needed something dramatic to work with, and I found it. What's wrong with her is our fault."

Martin stared back sharply.

"The old woman came out to the *Wasp* about twelve days ago on Hayden's invitation," Brandon said. "He showed her around his lab. Like we guessed, she lived up to the habits of all these backward savages and grabbed up one of the culture bottles because she thought it was pretty with the colored stuff inside it. It broke and cut her hand. She picked up the germ—or whatever. I'm no medic."

"Which culture bottle was it?" Martin's voice was reluctant because he was afraid of any answer.

Brandon's gaze was firm, meaning more than his words. "The one from the spikey plant we took two planets back. The one that killed that young botanist—Mason."

Martin was silent. He remembered the culture and the drab, lifeless planet which had produced it. Twelve days was the incubation period. It had taken twelve days for Mason to come down with it, and then Bowles had followed him, repeating the symptoms one day behind. Both botanists, they had both handled the spikey plant that transmitted the disease through innocent pricks. Mason had died. Bowles—.

Martin looked up, realizing why Brandon had given him that special stare.

"That's right," Brandon said. "You and Hayden saved Bowles,

Sunbear. It was trial and error all the way, but you two saved him. You know the right antidote."

"Of course!" Martin surged to his feet, starting immediately for the lab and the antibiotic they had used for Bowles. If he was in time, he could save Chantuka's wife. She was old and her resistance must be lower than Bowles', but if he hurried—.

"Just a minute," Brandon called him to a halt.

"I don't have a minute!"

"I said, 'Just a minute!'" Brandon assumed a tone that underlined his authority.

Martin came back.

"I've got orders for you, Sunbear. And they're full, command orders. You're not to tell Chantuka one word of this—understand? He isn't to know that we had anything to do with the disease. And when we save the woman, I want it stipulated that the treaty is the price. You're to help drive the point home."

"No." Martin said it flatly, cutting in on the end of Brandon's words. "You can't blackmail Chantuka with his wife's life."

"I have to." Brandon was dead sober.

"Not with *my* help. You shouldn't have told me you plotted this, Brandon. I won't go along with it. Not one filthy step. What would have happened if the bottle hadn't broken? Would you have injected her with it?"

"My motives are my business and go with my rank."

"But we should have started her treatment immediately! You knew that."

"She had to get good and sick for our plan to work. You and Hayden can start it now—with the treaty the condition for her cure."

"I will not agree to it," Martin spaced the words out and bit them off. "I won't abuse Chantuka this way. It's dirty. Did Evers know about it?"

"He did."

"And *he* went along with it?" Martin couldn't believe it of the missionary.

"He went along all the way. Why not, Sunbear? We've got the cure for her. A few days of being sick isn't too much to ask to seal the treaty. You just get underway and follow my orders."

Martin didn't move. Not one step.

"You're refusing my command?" Brandon demanded, his voice low.

"I am. Shoot me down where I stand—and right now—or I'll go and follow any course I think is decent enough, after what you've done." He stood still, waiting for Brandon's move, expecting a weapon to come out and put an end to the whole nasty affair.

Brandon let Martin's words register, then sighed, his face resigned to his frustration. "I don't execute my men. I'll leave that to your court martial. But be careful what you do because every action you take from this moment on goes into your record for prosecution. It's your choice." Suddenly his cold anger turned hot, and he cursed, "Dammit! What's so terrible about this? If we don't have the treaty, she'll die anyway! A lot of them will. When they're *forced* to come into line!"

Martin lifted the decorated material that served as a door, and stepped into the dim light of Chantuka's lodge. The chief was sitting on the sweet-smelling, grass-strewn floor by a low bed where his wife lay, gasping with her as she struggled for shallow, quick breaths. He was holding her hand in his own, engulfing it in a gesture of compassion and aching love.

The chief's son stood quietly in one corner, shadow-lit by the small fire that raised weak yellow flames in the center of the lodge. Tiva knelt by the fire, stirring some spicy brew in a large earth-colored pot. She looked at Martin once, then lowered her eyes, and her efforts at stirring told him more than her eyes had said. She was defeated and ready to grieve.

He had seen the same body expression in the people waiting outside, circling the lodge silently, caught in a still moment of time between faint life and creeping death.

Martin crossed to Chantuka and knelt beside him. He placed one hand on the old man's shoulder, then stared down at the woman. She was newly frail, her bronze skin glistening with the sweat of the disease, her eyes shut, her mouth slightly open to gasp in air.

Martin shuddered. He knew she was in pain because Mason and

Bowles had both cried out in their pain; but she was making no sound.

He turned away from the sight of her and focused on Chantuka. He began feebly, "I—I—. You know that I'm sorry—."

"You have no need to say it," Chantuka told him. The hand he cradled in his own was thin and weathered with sun and work, and he clung to it as though it was the source of his life. He spoke to Martin softly, his voice deep but never trembling. "I cannot understand this. It is something I have never seen. She has been suffering." He placed both of his hands about the woman's small one and pressed it gently, gathered a great breath for himself, and said, "Death will come soon, and then the suffering will end for her."

Martin's mind leapt to what he felt was a ridiculous thought in view of what he knew, but he voiced it anyway. "Has your medicine man tried everything he knows to heal her?"

Chantuka met his eyes. "No. That cannot be done. I could not allow him to try."

"But why?" Martin had to struggle to keep his voice low. If the medicine man could possibly succeed there would be no need for the blackmailed treaty.

"Mr. Evers has told me many times of the anger of your God and I have to admit that I fear it. He forbids me to call our medicine man."

"Forbids!"

"I understand the reasoning of it. As Mr. Evers said, once we have heard of the true God, then we are bound to follow His ways or accept His punishment. I—. I cannot endanger my people with a plague from this place, 'Heaven.' I cannot allow them to suffer because I am weak and do what Mr. Evers calls 'backslide.' Perhaps I am a coward, but I have thought about this for all these days of her sickness."

At that moment Martin wanted nothing more than to spit on Evers for putting terror into a heart which had never held any. He knelt beside the old man, himself as confused as Chantuka. In his own heart he felt strongly the sense of purity the medicine man would bring, yet he couldn't believe with certainty, he couldn't risk a life on his own heart's emotion. Hayden had a needle full of liquid that *was* certain, and even though it meant the sealing of a terrible treaty, it also meant the saving of Chantuka's wife. And the chief needed that saving more than

Martin Sunbear needed a demonstration of ancient religious purity.

"There is no other way for me than just to accept her death," Chantuka said. He was now strangely defiant, decision strengthening each line of his body. "She has had a long and happy life. She told me herself that she is content. Now, she sleeps. She will never wake."

Martin's eyes flashed with tears of pity and frustration and he stood up quickly, ready to tell Chantuka the truth about this disease and about Evers' Standardized God, but before he could speak a word, the lodge door lifted and Brandon strode in, followed by Hayden. The medic carried a medical kit.

Brandon started talking as soon as he was through the door. "I came back as soon as I could, Chantuka. Is she any better?"

Martin hated him for that question, but held his tongue.

Chantuka glanced up quickly at the intrusion, but only shook his head and whispered, "No. She cannot be."

"But she *can*," Brandon said. "Hasn't Sunbear told you about our plan for her? Our medicine?"

"I didn't have a chance," Martin told him, but Brandon's quick little sneer spoke paragraphs of snide understanding.

Brandon shoved his way in beside Chantuka. "Then I can be the one to give you the news, chief. There's a possibility that we can save your wife. Cure her. My crew and I." Brandon talked fast then, in his own simple grasp of the Kanan language, forcing Chantuka to understand that Hayden might be able to cure her with the wonderful power of Earth's medicines.

His explanation brightened Chantuka with its offer of hope, and the wrinkled face was suddenly eager. Chantuka rose to his feet to meet the captain eye to eye, searching Brandon's face as though he could read his sincerity right through his eyes.

Then Chantuka asked, "Martin Sunbear—is this all true? Should I let my heart be hopeful again?"

"It's true," Martin answered. "I was just ready to tell you when Captain Brandon came in."

"But I'm here now and I can handle it all," Brandon cut him short. "You just do the translating for me. This next part is essential." He swiveled suddenly to Hayden, "Call Mr. Evers. His Kanan is better than mine and he can check and see that Sunbear gets every word of what I say translated correctly."

Hayden moved quickly outside and Martin looked away, half turning his back, ashamed of what he knew he would have to speak in translation, and more ashamed of the fact that Brandon viewed him with such distrust that he had called for a watchdog.

Evers came in with Hayden and they all stood together in a tight little knot. Brandon cleared his throat meaningfully, spoke, and Martin swallowed his conscience and repeated the words, trying not to let them be a part of himself, trying to imagine himself as no more than the computer which could translate as well as he.

Brandon explained that he expected Chantuka's acceptance of their treaty if they did their best to restore his wife to him. Brandon didn't say, "If we *cure* her," but, "If we *try,*" crafty even in the wording of his betrayal. Martin translated those words, too.

The captain finished with a short, boasting pep talk about how the cure would prove to Kana once and for all time the worth of the things the galaxy had to give; their greatness and goodness.

As Martin finished his translation, something replaced the eagerness in the chief's attitude. Martin sensed it as desperate indecision and fear. By means of a single handclasp, Chantuka could save the life he valued most in the world; yet there was fear in him.

"Why are you holding back?" Brandon urged. "It's a simple and straightforward demonstration."

"I do not know," Chantuka spoke to Brandon, but gazed at Martin. "I feel that perhaps the two things cannot be weighed against each other—one life for a new and different future. I have a sense of foreboding."

They waited. The decision would be wholly Chantuka's. Whatever it was, Martin knew the woman would receive the treatment. Brandon couldn't keep him from that. He would inject the drug, himself.

He prayed silently that the Chief would refuse the bribe, then negated the prayer. The odds *had* to fall in Brandon's favor because there would be no future for the Kanans if they didn't.

Chantuka slowly paced the lodge, stopping once before Tiva and

once before his son. Their feelings were clear. They wanted the life—
their mother. He came back to Brandon and thrust his hand forward.
"Perhaps it is because I am old that I hesitate. I am alone in my fear.
I agree to let you try. Your people may come if your gifts prove good
for us."

Martin grabbed up the medical kit and set to work before Hayden
could even move to use his more professional knowledge. He motioned
to the pile of blankets Evers had brought. "Warm those," he told Tiva.
"Use stones—anything—but make them warm."

As the girl hurried to obey, he dug through the kit for the antibiotic that had saved Bowles' life. He thrust everything out of his mind
but the urgent need to battle a disease. The rest would have to come
later.

With the injection administered, he wrapped the frail old woman
in the warm blankets Tiva supplied, then gave over at Hayden's insis-
tence that he, as medic, should be in charge. Martin waited an hour in
the far corner of the lodge with Chantuka's son, then went out into the
center of the village.

The people were still there, still silent, and Martin picked out the
medicine man, Ro-gon, among them. He was sitting with the rest, but
with a difference about him. He wasn't simply waiting; he was agitated,
his hands moving in twitches, his body struggling to sit there patiently
when he hadn't been allowed to offer what he knew he had to offer.
Martin veered away from Ro-gon.

He roamed the edge of the waiting people, paced up a way into
the hills and came down again to reenter the lodge and check on the
woman's response to the antibiotic. But there was no response; not the
first time, nor the third. She lay just as before. Dying.

The hours dragged on with her gasps for breath, and they, in turn,
grew weaker. She wasn't responding, and Hayden frantically tried new
dosages, finally new methods, caught up, himself, in saving this life,
treaty or no treaty. Chantuka remained near her, never letting his hope
diminish, but Martin's hope plummeted. Something was wrong.

They had waited too long to start the treatment in the first place,
callously letting her go too deeply into the clutch of the disease, ignoring
the fact that she was old while Bowles had been young, that she had few

antibodies of her own to defend her because she had lived her life on a planet that was disease free. Martin had known when he gave the first injection that it had to start its work in a matter of a few hours or it would never control the bacterial invasion, and those few hours were running out.

Finally, he went to the *Wasp*, his feet shuffling in the Kanan grass. Brandon was waiting in the ship's tiny lounge. "Any change yet?" Brandon asked.

Martin shook his head.

"It's getting pretty late in the game, isn't it?" Brandon sighed. "Well—we made the deal on the basis of our *trying*, not our curing. We still have the treaty, either way."

"Good for us," Martin muttered, and went to his own quarters.

· It was dawn when Hayden returned, Evers behind him. They all met in the lounge. Hayden was exhausted, every line of his face deepened by the long day and night of working and watching. His first words were, "She's going to die. I can't stop it."

"You've given up?" Brandon demanded.

"I can't do anything else for her!" Hayden half shouted.

"I think we waited too long to begin," Evers put in.

"Is that the reason?" Brandon badgered Hayden.

"I don't know." Hayden slumped into a chair. "It could be. It's more likely the simple fact that she doesn't respond to our drugs in the same way we do. She's a different race. She's an alien. And she's dying. I came back to the ship because I didn't want to see the rest of it."

"And you?" Martin turned on Evers. "Didn't you stay to say your last words over her for Chantuka's benefit?"

Evers lashed back with the little strength he had left to muster, "I prayed for her all the time I stood in the litter-strewn shack."

"I thought you did," Martin spat. "But your god of vengeance decided to *take* some this time, right?"

Evers looked at him in confusion.

"Listen, Sunbear—," Brandon started.

"*You* listen," Martin cut him short. "You admit you've failed, right, Hayden? And you admit *you've* failed, right, Evers?"

They both stared at him blankly.

"I'm taking your silence for 'yes.' So now I'm free to try the only way that's left."

"What does that mean?" Brandon stood up, expanding his chest with his authority.

"Don't worry, I won't endanger your treaty. Just stay out of my way. I'm taking *my* right to a chance. I want that woman to live! I may fail, myself, but if I do, I damn well won't run away from her last gasps. I'll stay by Chantuka and give him whatever support I can!"

He left the lounge at a run and half slid down the ladder, heading full speed for the village and the thing he now saw clearly that he had to do.

He strode through the gathered Kanan people, only noting the exhausted, hopeless postures that had come upon them during the long night. It had become a death watch now and they were only sitting together to wait for it to fall.

He lifted the cover on Chantuka's lodge and stepped inside, halting his furious pace as the odor of sweat and pain and despair filled his senses. The lodge was dim. Tiva had let the fire burn itself down as her mother's life was burning down, and Chantuka's son had ceased his standing vigil to crouch in the corner, alone.

Chantuka turned from his place beside the bed and the old man's eyes were red and damp. "Thank you for coming, Martin Sunbear," he murmured. "But it still might be a long while. This death is slow."

Martin clasped the chief's shoulder, but with more urgency than sympathy. "We're not just going to wait for it, Chantuka. I've come to talk, and to find a way to help her."

"That is beyond us. Even your great medicine could not do it. Your Hayden poured out his heart in trying."

Martin clenched his teeth to force himself to speak the next words softly, "Our Hayden *caused* it, Chantuka. Our Hayden and our Brandon and our Evers."

The old man's tired mind couldn't comprehend, and Martin began to explain, slowly, in the best Kanan he could find, how the plot had been laid to infect the chief's wife, to let her sicken to the crisis point, and then bargain for the treaty with her life.

Chantuka showed one tall moment of shocked anger, his eyes glinting with fury. Then he said confidently, "You were not a part of this, Martin Sunbear."

"I was not. But I heard of it and I didn't tell you. I heard of it yesterday. After that, my only thought was to save her. I am ashamed. We've always had the truth between us."

"No." Chantuka rose from his place and strode to stand near the ebbing fire. "It is a dishonorable treaty, but *you* are not dishonored. I think I understand. It cannot matter now—anymore. I have made the treaty and *my* honor is good even though your fellowmen have none. I have lost, have I not. I was not wise enough to see into them."

"You haven't lost your wife yet, Chantuka. There is still hope for her. Use your *own way*. Call your medicine man."

Chantuka shrank away, ashamed to admit his fear. "Mr. Evers said that—."

"Forget what Evers said! His god is not yours. Call on your own god, Chantuka. Evers has no place in your mind at all. He *agreed* to this betrayal. He cannot be the holy man you thought he was."

The chief turned Martin's words in his mind, reluctant to decide too hastily again. He finally said, "You speak the truth. He could not be what I thought, and so his vengeful god may not be true, either. My duty then is to my wife. She has been the victim. Perhaps I can save her, at least." He swung to his son, "Ask Ro-gon to come to us. We will try our own way."

When Ro-gon, the tribal medicine man came, Martin quickly learned what methods he would use to attempt the cure, and as he heard, he felt hope seep into him, hope that came from ancient prayers and powers he had studied and stored secretly, but steadfastly.

He made a quick examination of the old woman and judged that death was still many hours away. Mason had gone through this stage of the disease and hadn't died for another twelve hours after its onset. If Ro-gon failed in his attempt, then her death would inch itself out to the end. But there *was* time to try.

He desperately wanted to make a request of Chantuka. He doubted if he had the right, but in the dim lodge, with the fire glowing down to its own death, he said softly, "Chantuka—may I stay and stand

with you? I'm not a member of your family—not even of your people
—but I want to add my soul to your prayers. I want it so much."

Now Chantuka was the one to clasp Martin on the shoulder. "You
are welcomed, and thanked. I am very tired, and your added strength
will help to fill my place."

Ro-gon interrupted. "What is your people's way, Martin Sunbear?
Can you adapt to ours?"

"The two ways are almost alike. I feel that I should purify myself,
but there isn't time. Even so, while you prepare, I'll go to the stream
and wash myself—get the dirt and feel of the *Wasp* off my body. I
promise not to make you wait. I'll be back before you begin."

He went from the lodge and paced through the people. This time
they were more alive in their faces. The sight of Ro-gon going to
Chantuka had given them new hope. They would sit together and pray,
now—silently, or perhaps aloud, in chants—but they knew they were at
last free to help.

Martin washed himself quickly in the cold water, letting the chill
cleanse more than his skin, and then the sun warm more than his body.
He didn't dress again. He only put on his trousers.

He pulled from his pocket a thing that he had always kept hidden
except at United Indian Nation meetings. It was a thin necklace of
sinew, and hanging from it was a painted leather symbol of the Sun
which was one representation of the Great Spirit. He put it on proudly,
and looking around himself at the beauty of this world, let the sense of
peace it brought wash him cleaner still.

Evers' angry voice broke his mood. "What have you done? I just
saw that witch doctor in Chantuka's shack. You've led that man to
backslide! After all my work! This can't be excused, Martin."

"Then, don't excuse it. Just get out of my way because I'm going
to join them in that 'shack' and cure that betrayed old woman."

Evers' eyes fell on the painted symbol. "That! That thing—!
You've lost your mind, Martin. What *is* that?"

"It's my cross, Mister Evers."

He started away, needing to hurry, but Evers was suddenly and
wildly up against him, grabbing at his arms, wrenching at him to hold
him back.

"I won't allow this, Martin!" Evers panted. "You've got to stop it right here!"

Martin grappled back, restraining himself from using all of his strength. He didn't want to hurt the slender missionary, but he had to break free. They tugged and pulled and then Martin thrust his full shoulder and weight into Evers, sending him backwards to sprawl on the ground, staring up, astonished.

"I'm sorry," Martin said. "But I'm following my own conscience. And I'm advising you and the rest of the crew to stay out of the village. The people won't be happy to see you right now."

The Kanans had positioned themselves in a perfect circle when Martin returned, and Chantuka's son and another man were edging slowly out of the lodge, carrying the bed with Chantuka's wife lying on it, eyes closed, her breast barely rising anymore as she had even stopped the hard gasping for breath. They placed the bed in the center of the circle, full in the sunlight, and the stranger took his place with the rest. Only Ro-gon, Chantuka's son, and Tiva remained on their feet. Chantuka was the last to appear from inside the lodge.

Martin went to the standing group hesitantly. He was out of place here and felt it, suddenly, but Chantuka took his arm and placed him in position facing the sun. Their shadows fell in long lines behind them, reaching like fingers into the crowd of silent Kanans.

Ro-gon approached him. The medicine man had not changed his clothing or put on any special symbols. He remained just as he had been, but there was something new in his posture—a confidence, a power—that emanated from him as he reached inside himself for the gift of understanding God had given to him. The power that allowed him to heal.

He spoke very softly to Martin. "You must release your spirit now, Martin Sunbear. Free yourself of your machines and potions and lift your mind to the True Source of help and love. As I look at you, I believe you can do this. I hope you succeed, because one false spirit could influence our work here. She is very old and very close to death."

"I understand," Martin answered him squarely. "And I know I can do it, Ro-gon, or I would never stand here with you. Your people are all of one mind now, and I'll join you in that. I am stripped down to my soul, and I think that soul is good."

"Your eyes say that it is," Chantuka murmured, and moved to stand closer to him.

For a moment, Martin wondered where he had found the simple words. There was something in the Kanan language, itself, something that described the world and its meanings in gentleness that allowed even an alienated man like himself to rise to the level of the true people around him.

He had little time to wonder at it because Ro-gon immediately walked to stand beside the old woman's bed. The Holy Man stared down at her for long, silent seconds, then raised his face to the sun, and all the faces in the circle around him lifted toward the sky.

It was time to begin.

Martin raised his own head, feeling the rays as heat, as tangible light on his cheeks and forehead, and his hand came up to clutch the symbol he wore against his chest.

Today he would make one sun out of two. Across the stars—one sun.

Ro-gon spoke to the sky and the wind. "We have brought Your daughter back into Your sunlight, Great Father, where she has lived and where You intend that she should always live. Take her back to Yourself again and let her open her eyes and breathe Your air gently as You commanded things to be many ages ago. She has suffered, but it was not of Your making. Your people gathered here know this. We ask now that You deliver her to us again, that her years may still be as You intended —loving, gentle, and good. We ask it with one voice—the voice of Your people.

"You placed Your hand on me in dreams and told me that I could speak these things for others. I am speaking them now. Great Father, Creator of all and Love of all, please hear us. Let Your daughter be well. Let the sun return into her life. We ask it, Great Father."

There was total silence over the village. Not even a bird called from the trees. Not an insect hummed in the grass. It was as if the world were waiting, staring to the sky, listening for an answer.

Martin waited, too, his hand tight on his painted symbol as he prayed "Great Spirit" and "God."

Then he closed his eyes because the sky was dazzling him with flecks of white and dancing motes. His mind tried to stray from the thought Ro-gon was expecting him to hold, and he heaved it back quickly. He knew this could take time. It might require hours of waiting and repeating. He would wait them out with the rest.

He couldn't tell time except by the feel of the sun slowly passing across his skin and the sky, but he judged it to be better than an hour before Ro-gon again cut the silence with his deep voice and called on the Great Father to imbue him with the gift He had bestowed on him in his dreams; to reach down for His daughter and let her know that life was still within her and her years were not yet spent.

"You ordained that she be happy, Great Father, and she was happy until this unknown thing fell upon her. And it is an unknown thing, since it is not of Your making. It cannot harm her or bring her to death since it is not of You. You do not harm. Your world and Your people are both gentle and good. Please whisper to her the truth once more so that she may open her eyes and draw safe breath. We all wait, Great Father, for Your choice. And this choice, of course, we will accept."

The silence came again.

But then it was broken by a soft murmuring from the gathered people. The murmur took form and grew into a quiet, repeated chanting. Over and over it sounded, in words that Martin didn't know. He listened and at last decided that they weren't really words at all, just round and quiet sounds. He should have known at once. These people would not repeat prayers aimlessly until they became nothing, meant nothing. The sounds, with their roundness and rhythm, were only manifestations of the spirits that were making them; praying, waiting. He quickly learned the pattern and joined the chant, hearing Chantuka take voice beside him.

"She sees!"

It was Ro-gon's voice that sliced the chant in two, and every head turned to look at Chantuka's wife.

It was true. The woman's eyes were open, gazing at the sky. She weakly turned her head to find Chantuka, but she didn't need to search long because he was beside her in three strides, kneeling down to touch her face with his own old hands.

"Breathe!" Ro-gon said.

Her expression was one of confusion and bewilderment, but she opened her lips and drew in a short, harsh breath; then raised her whole upper body in one great long sigh of life-giving air.

Chantuka cradled her face in his hands and leaned over her to lay his cheek against hers, hiding the tears that had started to course down his face.

And Martin breathed, too. All around him came a great sigh as the people breathed in and out with her. He hadn't realized he had been nearly holding his breath, but now the air hit his lungs clean and spicy with the touch of Kana.

Ro-gon stood where he had been and lifted his face to the sun again, smiling this time.

"Thank You, Great Father," he called, loudly, vibrantly. "Your people thank You for one more proof of Your great Love."

Martin felt tears on his own cheeks and suddenly wanted to get away from this place. The emotion was too much. The Power demonstrated here was too much.

He glanced at the old woman, noted that her color was beginning to return to her lips and fingers already, said a silent "Thank You" of his own, and walked out of the circle. He had no shadow as he walked now, because the sun was at its zenith. So he walked alone on the Kanan grass.

He had intended to wander and sort out his thoughts, but half a mile from the village he was met by an angry group, standing to watch him approach. He considered turning in the opposite direction, but decided against that. He could face them now. He had gained new power, himself.

Three men confronted him: Captain Brandon, Hayden, and an infuriated Mr. Evers. He wondered idly why Lyler never seemed to make himself part of anything that went on with the crew. But Lyler seldom had.

Brandon, as usual, was the first to open his mouth. "How come you've been free to fraternize down there, Sunbear, when you told Mr. Evers we should all stay out?"

"And how come you listened to me and *stayed* out?" Martin threw the question back without an answer.

"None of us are fools, Martin," Hayden said. "You're Alien Contact Officer so when you warn us about the natives, we believe you."

"I'm starting to think he's more *alien* than alien *contact,*" Brandon complained, eyeing Martin suspiciously. "So—what happened? Did the high mucky muck do his magic tricks and shake his rattles?"

Martin kept his tone quiet and level. "He saved Chantuka's wife."

Only Hayden, of the three of them, showed relief at the news. Brandon was confounded, his face red, his veins bulging.

Mr. Evers' whole skinny body was a fist of frustrated anger crying for a target. "That was probably the effect of Hayden's drugs—if it's true at all. The drugs undoubtedly just took effect."

"I don't think so," Martin answered. "But it doesn't matter. The point is, she's going to survive. Why aren't you happy about it, Mr. Evers? Can't you rejoice with the rest of her people?"

"*At what you did?* You—you—," Evers fought for expression, then it rushed out of him without any control. "Martin Sunbear, you led those people down the road to hell, do you know that? You took their hands out of mine, out of God's and the Standard Faith, without a thought to what you were doing to them. I *had* those people. They were ready. And now it will take so much to bring them back!"

"Back to what?" Martin asked, still quietly.

"To God, you foolish—you *fool!* They have to come. The treaty is made and colonies will be established and those savages have to fit in with us. They were ready!"

"Out of fear," Martin said.

"Out of an awakening in their souls of who God is and what He will do to them if they don't follow His commands. But you walked in there with that blasphemous painted—. You sent Chantuka back to his paganism—to pagan gods for a cure. You've made heathens out of them again. If I were a violent man—if I were given to physical force—."

"Go on and hit me, Evers. Just don't be surprised when I don't fall down. I've seen something today that I always knew existed but that I could never find. It was beautiful and it was true and it worked!"

"Paganism! Heathenism!"

"I don't care what you call it, Evers, but I saw God working. These people *have* God. Right here and now. A closer kinship with Him than you have. More understanding."

Evers scoffed, "Oh, come, Martin."

"Then how do you explain it? Hayden gave her all that our science can offer, but she was dying in spite of him. You prayed for that woman, Evers. You called on God's mercy for her, but she was dying in spite of *you.* One lone 'heathen' medicine man, uniting himself with God as he knows God, gave that woman back to her husband and children. I wasn't certain before that what I felt shoving me from the soul out was right, but now I *know!*"

Evers cut in, "You admitted you were raised in a rubbish pile of religion, Sunbear. Emotionalized Christianity plus your own redman's heathenism."

"Emotionalized Christianity? You're calling Christ's healings emotionalism, aren't you? Then, why did it work for her? I've read the old Bible, I've already admitted that. My parents gave it to me to read. And if you've read it, then you have to remember the passage where Jesus Christ said, *'He that believeth on me, the works that I do shall he do also.'* That includes healing, Evers. So I'm right according to what you call emotionalized Christianity.

"I'm also right according to the religion of my so-called redman ancestors. They healed, too, whether you like the idea or not. While they still had the Earth and their innocence and their faith, they could heal, too! I should have believed my own soul all along. I shouldn't have needed proof like I had this afternoon. But now I *know!*"

Evers met him anger for anger. "You're saying I'm a thing of the devil. That I'm evil and stupid and soulless."

"I'm saying nothing of the sort. Your intentions are only good, Evers, and I realize that. Your own heart is decent, but you're bent on destroying a perfect people and their pure relationship with God in spite of that—just because they happen to worship Him differently and call Him by a different name.

"One God is one God, Evers. And they already have Him. Just as my people had Him. I won't let you force them to lose Him and then spend the rest of eternity trying to struggle their way back Home!"

"The Kanans have no choice, Martin!" Evers was shocked at his harangue. "You can't stop the treaty from proceeding to its final end, and if the Kanans don't adapt to our colonials, they're going to be physically injured. Perhaps destroyed! So what you're demanding for them—this insulation—can only be brought about in one way. Are you going to ask them to follow that one way? To commit racial suicide as your brother Navajos tried to do? Do you actually want their *blood* just because of a lack of roots you feel in yourself, Martin?"

Martin stood perfectly still, his mind and body rolling in a great surge of emotion. Evers had hit the sorest spot of all. He was falling to pieces right in front of the three of them and he had no place to hide. They could never understand what he meant.

He grasped the painted symbol again, drew a shivering breath, and said only, "Forget the 'Martin.' My name is Sun Bear. A true and old Dakota name."

He spun around and paced away, then ran, needing the haven of his favorite hillside near the village to still his mind and help him evaluate what had happened to him and whether or not Kana could possibly be saved.

The hill held the same serenity it had always held, but he couldn't respond to it. He was too hard pressed, attacked from too many sides by doubts and terrors about his own motives and about Kana's future.

Memories and stories pulled at him, taking him back through years he had never seen to days he only knew through books and legends told at UIN meetings. Why should they be so real? What had happened to him here on Kana? Something terrible had happened and he wanted to stamp it all down, strangle it, bury it, deny it completely. Those days weren't his to own, but they were twisting him apart.

He moved into the shade of an arching tree where birds whisked in and out of the heavy-leafed branches, piercing the day with pipings. He cast his eyes down onto the village. There was so much inside him that wanted to be part of that village, to live in a past he had believed dead—but he had no place there. No right there. He had helped save

Chantuka's wife, but even that act had only required convincing the chief to call on Ro-gon. He had stood with them in the healing prayers, but it would have been done without him just as well.

So he still had no home.

And as he looked at it objectively, from this higher vantage point, his body pressed against the grass and a large winged butterfly making flirting passes at the blue color of his trousers, he stilled the aching the scene brought to him. Stilled it deliberately.

This was not a hillside on the plains of Earth. He did not wear feathers in his hair. He did not ride a painted horse. That was gone. Forever. Tatters of it appeared at the UIN meetings, but they were tatters and nothing more. So he had to accept the rest of his life as it came to him. He would have to remain an alien among his own kind; a homeless man, keeping his own counsel.

Grief broke over him and he shuddered with it.

The village below took on the look of a stage with a pantomine being played out for him. Pitifully, he already knew the climax.

The people were busy, streaming in and out of their lodges, slowly changing before him from their normal clothing to brighter colors—to decorations, to ornaments—and he understood, at last, that they were preparing for a celebration, a time of thanksgiving for the life that had been given back to them.

Thanksgiving!—while their fate was still sealed tight in Brandon's and Chantuka's handclasp. The treaty was made. Colonists would come and dig into Kana, sending their machines down into the ground to scoop out foundations for wooden houses that would eventually turn to plastic when it could be manufactured in new factories supplied by the ore the new miners produced.

Evers would also have his way. The Standard Faith would be taught—that hodgepodge that really meant nothing. The Kanans would have to adapt themselves in order to be absorbed and changed into images of the larger civilization. If they didn't, they would meet fear, hatred, prejudice, and be abused.

If he told Chantuka the truth about the future, then the old chief in his outraged honor would deny the treaty and be faced with an invasion he didn't even know could come.

There was no way out. Only destruction lay at the end of every course. And he, Martin Sunbear, hadn't helped at all.

He watched the village and allowed the sight to lull him into feeling part of it, enjoying the bright clothes, the ornaments, because it was the last time he would see it. When the *Wasp* left Kana, he would never come back again.

He was soothed by the hill and the birds and the village until the afternoon had almost worn away. Time slipped by him as he conjured drum beats to go with the rising smoke of cooking fires and composed songs to sing at the thanksgiving ceremonies.

Then some women came partway up the hill, gathering flowers and grasses for the celebration, and they woke him from his revery. As he watched them work and admired their necklaces of shells and tiny feathers, another stab slapped through him.

Among those natural decorations he caught sight of cheap jewelry from his own culture; plastic combs, glass necklaces of many colors glinting in the sunlight, wristwatches that were given out simply as pretty bracelets and had no working parts.

"Insidious!" he cried, and was on his feet before he realized it. The woman looked up at him, but he turned his back.

He paced further up the hill, hating himself for the wasted time, for accepting defeat. He might not ever return to Kana, but the destruction would occur just the same. Here he stood in the position where no one had stood when his own ancestors needed help. He wouldn't turn his back. He had to find a way to stop the ruin. *There had to be a way!*

He would wrestle with his mind on this hill until he found it.

When he returned to the *Wasp* it was dusk, the day almost drained away, but his step was firm and quick, his strength full, because he had found a plan and the new Sun Bear could do anything necessary to preserve this adopted culture, withstand anything Brandon might throw at him, hold his own emotions close—anything—to win his argument and convince Brandon of the good in the one way he had found.

The *Wasp* sat with its nose in the air, spotlights making a bright circle around it as the night gathered. Martin climbed the ladder to the lock and went inside. He found Brandon alone in the radio room, grateful that he was alone. He had to have the captain to himself if there was going to be any chance for this at all.

Brandon was working on some papers and when he looked up his face was immediately hostile. "Where'd you go? Off to beat your tom-toms?"

"Off to think," Martin said, putting humility into his voice.

Brandon's hostility began to fade. "Good. And since you came back to the *Wasp*, I take it you've made the right decision. I'm glad, Sunbear. I hate to see a good officer go alien crazy. So—rejoin the crew and come to our party. We're breaking out everything we've got tonight. It's time to whoop, boy."

"You couldn't really want me after this afternoon," Martin played on with his humility. "Not after what I did."

To his surprise, Brandon showed a little tooth in a smile. "You got carried away. So what? I've seen it once or twice before. Alien crazy. You contact men sometimes go slightly mad. I can understand that. Carried away. Hell, I'm carried away, myself! I can barely wait out the hours until the *Astra's* in position and I can get on that radio and tell them what we've done down here. This is *big*, Sunbear. The biggest planet find we've made. So untouched and all here for us. It's going to guarantee my future. Yours, too."

"I don't want any credit," Martin said evenly.

Brandon dropped his pencil and spread his hands on the papers he was preparing, clearly deciding to ignore the edge he had heard in Martin's voice. "Give yourself some time. You're no more a savage than I am."

When Martin made no reply, Brandon continued, actually trying to make excuses for him. "You've been edgy all through this contact, Sunbear. I've seen it. I'm not a captain for nothing, you know. And— I'm willing to forget it happened. This once. Agreed?"

Martin hesitated. This was the moment to make his beginning, but he didn't know how. He could only find one way; bluntly, and with the whole truth. "It's not agreed, captain. I'm sorry. I said I'd been thinking. The trouble is, I didn't come to the conclusions you think I did. I don't like the treaty. We shouldn't interfere with these people."

"Interfere?" Brandon snatched at the word, caught off balance by what he had believed to be a reconciliation and had now turned sour on him. "Since when has contact for mutual advancement been called interference?"

"It will change their entire way of life."

"Of course it will. It will lift them right up off their skins and flowers and put them in the space age." He eyed Martin closely. "This thing's still eating you up, isn't it? Well, tell me what's in your head, Sunbear. I really do want to know."

Now was his time to catch Brandon's mind or lose it. "The Kanans will never be able to stand against our civilization, captain. This isn't an ordinary culture. Not anything like the ones we usually find. We'll introduce things here that have never been here before—lust, greed— all of our sins and more. We have no right to contaminate it."

"That part of it's up to Evers and his kind. Don't be a fool, Sunbear. These people are ripe. And who are we to say 'no' when they want us?"

"They don't know what they're doing."

"We can't even talk anymore, can we? You've got steel inside your brain and it won't budge an inch. Give Chantuka some credit. We told him what we have to offer and he wants it. All we want to do is *give* it to him. To all of them. We'll give a thousand times more than we gain."

It was starting to go wrong, but Brandon's mind was still slightly open, so Martin sucked in his breath and went wholly on the offensive. "So far we've given them gambling, rape, and the near death of a beloved old woman."

"That wasn't my fault. How was I to know about the drug resistance? She didn't die. Even if she had, one death is better than genocide. And the future we'll give them will more than compensate for—."

Martin whirled on him, his voice hollow, "There are times when 'giving' is not appropriate, Brandon; when it's more 'taking away.' When it's a benevolent, but insidious destruction. If they really knew what's in your hands, maybe they wouldn't want what you've got."

Brandon's own voice was suddenly quiet and calm. "Now it's what *I've* got? You're dropping out of the picture again? Just when did this total alienation happen, Sunbear?"

"I don't know. Maybe two hundred years ago when my own people were given the 'great gifts' of an advanced civilization. When they discovered that they had to trade dignity and God for felt hats with feathers sticking in them!" He forced himself to hold in, and went closer to Brandon. "I want to save these people from that fate. I want to do for them what no one did for us. I'm asking you to help me."

Brandon was too dumbfounded, and too nervous because of his proximity, to give a sensible answer. "You *are* crazy. Just *plain* crazy!"

"Try to understand. Please. This is something I have to do and I can't help myself. I've cooperated with you all the way so far. Now I'm pleading with you to go along with *me*."

Brandon made a valiant attempt to make his voice soothing. "Look, Sunbear, I can't do anything. Without the treaty, there will be invasion for them. You don't want that, and there's no way around it."

"There *is* a way. The one thing that makes a planet off-limits to us forever. Quarantine! We can report that Kana isn't safe. We can quarantine Kana so no one else will ever come here. The other men will go along, I think. They've liked it here too much to want to hurt these people. I'm positive of Hayden. And Lyler and Evers can be persuaded."

"That's treason!" Brandon dropped his pretense and let the words roar out.

"But it will work, captain. Once a planet is quarantined, no one else ever comes to it. That's the law! And we can stay here. We're not important, anyway. The issue overshadows us."

Brandon shook his head. "Your plan defeats your own purpose. Having us around would be just as influential to the natives as having colonials around."

"We can risk that. At least there's a chance my way. Your way, there's nothing."

"No, Sunbear, it's out of the question. You're sick—not responsible—but you're wrong. You're a total misfit. *You* don't care if you ever go home or not. But, I do!" Brandon suddenly darted to the left and jammed his fingers on the red emergency button.

With the quick motion, Martin almost responded out of panic, almost attacked, but stopped himself short. The alarm sounded, screaming through the ship, and immediately the clank of answering feet pounded over their heads.

"There was no need for that," Martin said. "I'm not going to attack you, Brandon."

Hayden and Lyler appeared at the door, but Brandon motioned them to stay outside. "Now, Sunbear—do I lock you up for the rest of our stay? Or do you behave yourself?"

"No!—no lockup," Martin muttered. His mind was racing, trying to sort possibilities. All he knew was that he had to remain free. "I won't bother you anymore. You have all the cards, anyway. I can't hurt you. I know that and so do you."

Brandon looked hard at him, then shrugged. "For once, you're right. Just be here when it's time to radio the *Astra*. I want some sign from you that you're still a member of this crew."

"You'll have it. I'll be beside you all the way." He left, brushing past Lyler and Hayden who were still tensed for trouble. They let him pass.

He arrowed straight for Chantuka's village. Reporting Kana unfit for habitation was still the only way out. Brandon had blocked it, but it was still the only way. And he was still the only one who was willing to do it.

As he came to the edge of the village, he decided one thing surely. He would tell Chantuka the truth about Kana's actual choice in the treaty. If nothing else, he had to relieve his conscience of the lies.

The old chief met him at the doorway of his lodge, but Martin brushed by him and entered gravely, only nodding hello to Tiva. Then, giving the chief no chance to speak, he rushed right into the tale of treachery he had to tell.

Chantuka listened with his eyes wide at first, then his face closed down, revealing nothing. But when Martin finished, Chantuka exploded in protest. "How could anyone do that? They would actually come in great numbers and kill us? No! How could anyone be so cruel?"

Martin looked at the grassy floor of the lodge. He couldn't explain this to Chantuka any more than he had really managed to explain the dead rabbit to Tiva.

Chantuka protested a moment more, and then stopped, accepting what he had heard whether he understood it or not. There was only sadness in him, all directed at Martin. "It was hard for you to go along with those things. And even harder for you to tell me about them. I thank you for your courage."

"It didn't do either of us any good," Martin answered.

"No. The wicked men have won this time. But I have made the treaty, so I must stand by it."

"And you would, because of honor and everything else you believe in," Martin said, and it was almost a curse. "It's still up to me to keep you from being destroyed."

"But you have already tried. Your captain said no to your plan."

"It was a true plan, even so. And it still is!" Martin met Chantuka's eyes for the first time since he had entered the lodge. "Chantuka—will you trust me enough to do as I ask?"

"I would have to be made of rock not to trust you now."

"Then—one question. If I do what I have in mind to do, the crewmen will be very angry. They might even try to harm you. How would you handle that?"

"We would defend ourselves as we always do against wicked men," Chantuka said. "We would have to send them to the Judgement Place."

Martin's skin grew cold. "And this place? Is—is it a place of dying, Chantuka? Would they be killed? I don't—."

"The Judgement Place is not for killing, Martin Sunbear. It is only a place apart. Do you understand? A place where the wicked ones go to be kept away from the people. They are not harmed. Not even physically restrained."

Now it was Martin's turn not to understand.

Tiva spoke up, "It is the place for the ones who are not willing, for the ones who do evil things." She laughed, looking to her father, "Martin Sunbear thinks we are all good on Kana, father. I know that from my talks with him."

"All good?" Chantuka smiled a little. "That would be impossible. Sometimes we find a wicked one, and then he must go to the Judgement Place. There he is in the hands of God. He has all he needs in food and shelter. Unfortunately, he even has companionship since there are others who have been sent there before him. But he is not allowed to come back among us."

"We keep a watch, even so," Tiva finished the explanation. "To be sure all is well with them."

"Of course! Ostracism! I should have guessed. My own ancestors practiced ostracism." Martin sighed, relieved. "That leaves my way clear, then. I can follow my plan. Again, Chantuka—will you trust me?"

"There is no need for you to ask. Yes, I will trust you."

"Then, listen carefully. We haven't much time. I'm going back to the *Wasp* and a few minutes after I leave, I want you to come to the ship with every man in the village. I want you to make a loud noise about it. Act angry, threatening—anything you can think of that will draw the crew out of the *Wasp*."

"But why?" Chantuka asked simply.

"To give me time alone inside. There is only one way to save your world, and I'm going to take it."

"Then—we shall help you. Trust *us*, now."

With Chantuka's words, he left, running the distance to the *Wasp*. It was quiet inside the ship and he didn't go to Brandon. Let the captain think he was still gone. When the time came, Brandon would know he was there in capital letters. He went into his own cabin, leaving the door ajar so he could hear. It wasn't many minutes before a low, buzzing sound came from outside the *Wasp*, and grew until it was discernible as the shouts of men.

Brandon's voice echoed in the metal corridor, "Somebody find out what the devil's going on out there!"

Footsteps hammered to the lock and Hayden shouted, "It's the whole village coming, captain. They've got clubs in their hands."

"Where's Sunbear?" Brandon hollered. "Sunbear!"

"I'm here." Martin strode into the corridor. Everyone was by the outer lock, watching the mob of Kanans who were coming, waving their clubs and shouting angry Kanan words.

"What do you make of this?" Brandon demanded.

"I can't make anything of it. They've never been hostile, you know that."

"Then they're probably not hostile now? Is that what you're saying?"

"They look it, but I doubt if they intend anything," Martin hedged.

"Our first duty is to protect the ship," Brandon decided. "We'll just get out there and—."

"You wouldn't use weapons on them!" Martin gasped. His plan couldn't backfire against Chantuka now.

Brandon hesitated—then, "No—no I suppose not. We'll try to talk first, but if it turns out to be necessary, you're going to lose some of your blessed 'brothers.'" Brandon's eyes were mean. "Everybody outside. Act friendly, but stand firm."

Martin hung back while the four men exited the ship. As Lyler's foot left the ladder and touched ground, Martin shut the door and locked it. The crew of the *Wasp* was outside—locked out by sheer, bare metal—and he was alone to do what had to be done. He laughed to himself as he went to the radio room. Chantuka had managed to look more menacing than he had thought possible.

Sudden pounding on the outside of the ship didn't stop him. Brandon wanted back inside. But Brandon wouldn't get back inside. Not until the *Astra* had been contacted and the false report given. He sat down at the radio, warmed the apparatus for sending, and waited out the final minutes before contact time. The pounding on the hull continued for a while and then stopped. But he was certain the men were safe in Chantuka's hands, so he paid no attention. They would live, every one of them—simply cut off from all fraternization.

The minutes went by and contact time ticked up. He opened the switches and called into the radio, *"Astra—Astra—this is the Wasp."*

"Brandon?" a tinny voice asked after a long minute's wait. "This is the *Astra*. Is that you, Brandon?"

Martin braced himself for the final lie. "This is Martin Sunbear of the *Wasp*. Brandon is dead. They're all dead! I'm the only one left alive. Repeat—the crew is dead. This planet harbors a plague. Quarantine!" His voice shook with the lie and the knowledge that he was condemning Brandon, Lyler, Hayden and Evers to spending their lives here, to never seeing home again. But he wanted the tremors in his voice. They gave credence to his next words. "The fever's rising in me now. This is the only report I'll be able to make. This planet is death. Men cannot survive here. Repeat—*cannot survive!*"

"Sunbear!" the tinny voice cried. "For God's sake—everyone else is dead?"

"Everyone."

"Is there anything we can do for you, man? Any way we can get you off in time to—."

"Nothing," Martin gasped into the radio. "We tried everything in the medical book. There's nothing to be done—except to keep other men away from here. We couldn't even find the cause—not even the cause. Just place the quarantine and—."

"Of course. But, you! What about you?"

"I'm dead, *Astra*. Just place the quarantine. I'm signing off. I won't be calling again."

He switched off immediately, haunted by the compassion in the tinny voice from the *Astra*. He set about destroying the radio systematically, making sure there would never be a way to repair it. Then he destroyed the spare parts—and he was finished. The lie had gone out and no one would ever come to Kana again. No one. And no one would ever leave Kana, for without the radio, they couldn't home in on the *Astra*.

He waited in the corridor, catching his breath, feeling like a traitor and a savior at the same time. Brandon and the crew had to be faced and told. He would take their abuse and deserve it. But he had saved his half-home. And he could live out his life at least partially content, millions of miles from the Earth that had never fostered contentment in him.

He opened the outer lock and stepped into the spotlighted night, meeting the native faces that stared up at him blankly, searching out Chantuka. The old chief stood at the foot of the ladder and Martin went halfway down to talk to him.

"It's done," Martin told him. "I've arranged it so that you'll never be bothered by us again. That is a promise." He glanced about, ready to hear Brandon's curses, but Brandon and the other men weren't in the crowd. "Where is the captain?" he asked.

"I sent your fellowmen to the Judgement Place," Chantuka said, his face more lined than Martin had ever seen it.

"Already?"

"It was best not to wait and let them grow angry enough to injure someone—or themselves. I was sorry to do it, but we agreed, you and I, and I explained it to my people and they accepted it, too."

Martin sighed deeply, now having to say a thing he didn't want to say, but determined to follow his course honestly and honorably. "Then—I must join them."

He felt oppressed by the night. The sweet future he had won for these people was smothering him. He hung onto the railing, decision sure and final in him, but tearing at him in spite of the rightness of it. "I'll go now, if you'll have someone show me the way."

"No!" Chantuka cut in quickly. "That is not for you. You are not unwilling or wicked. You belong free with us."

Martin's heartbeat quickened with a sudden yearning, but he wouldn't allow it to influence him. "And now it's my turn to say 'no.' You have to understand one thing, Chantuka, and understand it well. Keep to yourselves—entirely. That even means to keep away from *me!* Don't ever give up anything you have to anyone. If you change with the years, let it be your *own* change. If you are ever visited again by some other alien race, don't offer that first ear of corn."

"Corn?" the wrinkled face was puzzled.

"Don't offer anything; and don't accept anything. The greatest gift any other civilization has to offer you is Nothing. You cannot benefit through them. You can only be hurt."

Chantuka nodded his white-haired head, understanding. "But what of you, Martin Sunbear? The man who saved us must stay with us. You need not go off with your comrades. I have seen it in your eyes that this is truly your home. It is strange, but I think perhaps you are one of us—inside. You could not, and *would* not hurt us."

Martin Sunbear clutched the railing hard. This choice was an unbearable one. Every pore of him cried out to accept Chantuka's welcome, but he didn't know if he should. He wanted it more than he had wanted anything in his life.

He raised his eyes to the dark sky and watched the wings of a night bird beat the soft air near the spotlights, and as the bird called, high and pure, he let the truth come out of himself, confident that he was following the right path.

He said, as he looked back to meet Chantuka's eyes, "I believe it, too. In fact, I *know* it. I *can* live with you by watching myself closely so that I never influence you. I vow this—here where I stand. The first time I see myself influencing you, I will go and stay where Captain Brandon is. Forever."

Chantuka reached up and took his hand from the railing, pressing it firmly, sealing the vow. "That day will never come. And you will be a great man among us and become a legend. You will never be forgotten in our history. If strangers come, they will not be welcomed innocently again. We will be hard and isolate them before they can strike us. They will offer gifts, but the memory of my people is long, and they will always be compared to the man who saved us. The man-who-offers-gifts will never stand above the man-who-offered-nothing."

Martin Sunbear humbly stepped down into the crowd of Kanans to become one of them. His conscience about Brandon and the others would ease, and he'd personally see to it that they were all right. There was nothing to hurt them on this world, anyway.

As he walked tall and straight with his new people, he thought that it was strange to find that even a span of two hundred years had not been able to quiet the pound of blood and tradition that raced through his veins. He was stripped of all acquired civilization now. He could throw it off gratefully, knowing that when a man is so much alone, he goes back to what is true inside him.

Perhaps no one would ever understand why he had done it. They didn't matter.

Perhaps the god of the galaxy would not understand. But that didn't matter.

The God of Sun Bear would know—the Great Spirit, the kind and mighty God of the old times; the God Who lived with Kana.

The few who knew about the brotherhood of life would understand; and the soul of Tiva's little rabbit; and the spirits which had once belonged to bones that lay in ancient Earth, strewn with the remnants of eagle feathers.

towards the beloved city

BY PHILIP JOSÉ FARMER

The western sky was as red as if it had broken a vein. In a sense, it had, Kelvin Norris thought.

The Earth had broken open too, and it was this which had created the bloody sunsets. The Pacific and Mediterranean coasts had shaken many times with a violence unknown since the days of creation. Old volcanoes had spouted, and new ones had reared up. It would be twenty years before all the dust would settle. It would have been a hundred years if it had not been for the great nightly rains, rains which nevertheless did not succeed in making the atmosphere wet, at least, not along the Mediterranean coast. By noon the air was as dry as an old camel bone, and at sunset the sky was red with light reflected from the dust that would not die.

A thousand years would have to pass before the dust of human affairs would settle. Meanwhile, this land was tawny and broken, like the body of a dead lion torn by hyenas. And the sun, rising after last night's violent rain, had been another lion. But it lived, and its breath turned the skin of men and women to leather and burned the bones of the dead to white. Even now, sinking towards the horizon, it lapped greedily at the moisture in Kelvin Norris's skin.

He was riding a horse, the only one he had seen alive since he and his party had landed near the submerged city of Tunis. There were many bones of horses and other animals, killed in the quakes or by tidal waves or bombings or gunfights or by disease or by starving men, for food. Bones of men also lay everywhere. The crows and ravens and kites were, however, numerous, though swiftly losing their fat now. Kelvin knew the taste of their stringy carrion-smelling flesh very well.

The party had traveled on foot from the California mountains across the continent, had built from wreckage a small sailing ship with an auxiliary engine, sailed across the Atlantic to England and from there down along the newly-created coasts of France and Portugal, through the straits of Gibraltar (past the great tumbled rock), and then had been wrecked by a storm on the shore of what was left of Tunisia.

Three days ago, Anna Silvich had shot a scrawny goat; that had kept them from collapsing with hunger. Then Kelvin had found the white stallion, which was amazingly sleek and healthy. Its presence, so well fed, in these bleak and deserted environs, seemed a miracle. Some of the party said that it *was* a miracle. Perhaps this was the very horse on which the rider called Faithful and True had led the hosts of heaven to victory over the Beast and the Antichrist.

But Kelvin said that he did not think that was likely, though it could be one of the horses ridden by one of the hosts that had followed the Faithful and True into the final battle. However, if a miracle were to be performed, it would be just as easy to transport them, teleport them rather, in the closing of an eye, the scratching of a nose, instead of letting them slog along by boat and foot. But this was not to be; they were alone. He hastened to add, as the others frowned, that he meant that the party would never be alone, of course, in the sense that He was always with them. What he had meant was that they could not just sit down and expect some sort of celestial welfare.

That morning, Kelvin had taken a rifle and thirty bullets, all he had for a .32 caliber gun, a goatskin waterbag containing distilled water (which became red-colored two hours afterward), and a leather sling and some stones, and had ridden into the hills. The countryside here had been stripped by the cataclysms, but, in the past three years, some plants had reestablished themselves. There were still hares and rodents and lizards and the little desert foxes in this area. He hoped to get some of these with his sling. The .32 was for protection only or in case he should, by some chance, find larger game.

He had tied the horse to a bush and had gone on foot into the tumbled and deeply-fissured hills. He smashed a lizard with a stone from his sling and dropped it into the bag hanging from his belt. A few minutes later, he killed a raven with a stone. And then, under a deep shelf of rock, he found the ashes of a recent fire and some thoroughly scraped sheep and rat bones. There were no tracks in this rocky wilderness for him to follow, but he went down three long fissures searching for signs of the fire-builder. Reluctantly, he gave up looking and returned to the place where he had tied the horse. His tightening belly and his weakness told him that he would have to give permission for the horse to be butchered. It would hurt him to kill such a fine animal, but the party would then have plenty of meat for a few days.

The ringing of iron shoes on rocks warned him before he left the mouth of the fissure. Crouching, he looked around a boulder. A woman with short curly auburn hair, dressed in a ragged and dirty green coverall, was riding his horse away.

He did not want to shoot her or to make the horse bolt because of the shot. He put the rifle down and ran out after her while he took a stone from the bag at his belt and fitted it into the sling. She turned her head to look behind her just as the stone gave her a glancing blow on her back, near the spine. She screamed and fell forward off the horse; it reared and then galloped off.

Kelvin approached her with the rifle pointed at her. She seemed to be armed with only a knife, but he had learned long ago not to trust to appearances. At the moment, she did not look as if she could use a hidden weapon, even if she had one. She was sitting up, leaning on one arm, and groaning. The skin on her arms and legs and on one side of her face was torn.

"Any broken bones?" he said.

She shook her head and moaned, "Oh, no! But I think you almost broke my back. It really hurts."

"I'm sorry," he said, "but you were stealing my horse. Now, take out your knife slowly and throw it over to one side. Gently."

She obeyed and then slowly got to her feet. At his orders, she stripped and turned around twice so that he could make sure that she had no weapons taped to her. After he inspected the coverall, he threw it back to her, and she put it back on.

"Have you got anything to eat?" she said.

"The dinner ran away," he said. "What's your name and what are you doing here? And are you a Christian?"

There had been a time when he would not have asked that last question. He had assumed that all those who had bowed to the Beast and allowed it to put its mark on them had been killed either during the series of cataclysms that had almost wrecked the Earth or during the war afterwards. But it had long been evident that he had misread the Revelation of John.

"I'm Dana Webster of Beverly, Yorkshire, and I was in a party which was going to the beloved city. But they're all dead now, mostly of starvation, though some were killed by heathens. I found the horse, and I took it because I wanted to get away from whomever owned it, far away, where I could eat the horse without worrying about being tracked down."

She did have a slight English accent, he noted. And her remark about the heathens implied that she was Christian. But she could retract the statement, or rationalize it, if it turned out that she had given the wrong answer. After all, she had no way of knowing that he was really a Christian.

He handed her his canteen, and she drank deeply before giving it back. "It tastes wonderful, even if it does look like blood," she said. "Do you suppose it'll ever get its natural color back? I mean, its lack of color."

"I don't know," he said.

"There's a lot we don't know, isn't there?"

"We'll know when we get to the beloved city," he said. "Let's go."

She turned and walked ahead of him. He carried the rifle in the crook of his elbow, but he was ready to use it at any time. They trudged along silently while the sun dropped through its pool of red. Once, he thought he saw the east begin to lighten, and he stopped, giving a soft cry. She halted and then turned slowly so that he would not misinterpret her movement.

"What is it?" she said.

"I thought . . . I hoped . . . no . . . I was mistaken. I thought that the east was beginning to light up with His glory and that He was surely coming. But my nerves were playing tricks on me. Nerves plus hunger."

"Even if you saw a glory wrapping the world," she said, "how do you know that it would be Him? How could you be certain that it was He and not the Antichrist?"

He goggled at her for a moment and then said, "The Antichrist and the Beast went into the flaming lake!"

"What Beast? I thought the Beast was the world government? You surely don't mean that mythical monster that Gurets was supposed to have locked up in a room in his palace? As for the flaming lake, has anyone ever seen it? I know no one who has. Do you? Actually, all we know is what we've heard by word of mouth or the very little that comes over our radio receivers, supposedly from the beloved city. And where is the beloved city? Well, actually, there isn't any, as the broadcaster admits. There is a site somewhere in what used to be mountainous Israel where the faithful will gather and where the beloved city will be built by the faithful under the supervision of, I presume, angels.

"But how do you know that all this is true or why we're being led, somewhat like sheep into a chute, towards the beloved city? And if there is a flaming lake, and God knows there are plenty all over the world now, how do you know that the Antichrist went into it? Wouldn't the Antichrist, or whoever is supposed to be the Antichrist, have spread this tale about to make the faithful think it was safe to come to Israel?"

"You must be a heathen!" Kelvin said. "Telling a lie like that!"

"Do you see any numbers on my hand?" she said. "And if you looked at my forehead with a polarizer, you wouldn't see any numbers there, either. And if you care to, you can look at my scalp. You won't see any scars there because my head wasn't opened and there's no transceiver there for the Beast to activate any time it wants to press a button."

"We'll see about that when we get to camp," he said.

"I'm not telling lies," she said. "I'm just speculating, as any Christian should. Remember, the Serpent is very cunning and full of guile. What better way to fight those who believe in God than to pose as Christ returned?"

Kelvin did not like the path down which his mind was walking. There should be no more uncertainties; all should be hard and final.

Things were not what he had thought they would be. Not that he was reproaching God even in his thoughts. But things just had not worked out as he had assumed they would. And his assumptions had been based on a lifetime of reading the Scriptures.

"Were you one of those martyred by the Beast?" he said.

Dana Webster had started walking again. She did not stop to reply but slowed down so that he was only a step behind and a step to one side of her.

"Do you mean, was I one of those whose heads were rayed off and who was then resurrected? No, I wasn't, though I could easily claim to be one and no one could prove that I was lying. Most of my brothers and sisters were killed, but I was lucky. I got away to a hideout up on Mount Skiddaw, in Cumberland. The Beast's search parties were getting close to my cave when the meteorites fell and the quakes started and everything was literally torn to shreds."

"God's intervention," he said. "Without His help, we would all have perished."

"Somebody's intervention."

"What do you mean by *somebody?*"

"Extraterrestrials," she said. "Beings from a planet of some far-off star. Beings far advanced beyond man—in science, at least."

The ideas from her were coming too fast. "Could Extraterrestrials resurrect the dead?" he said.

"I don't know why not," she said. "Scientists have said that we would be able to do it in a hundred years or so, maybe sooner. Of course, that would require some means of recording the total molecular makeup and electromagnetic radiation patterns of an individual. That would someday be possible, according to the scientists. And then, using the recordings, the dead person could be duplicated with an energy-matter converter. This was also theoretically possible."

"But the person would be duplicated, not resurrected," he said. "He would not be the same person!"

"No, but he would think he was."

"What good would that do?"

"How do I know what superbeings have in their superminds? Do you know what's being planned for you by God?"

He was becoming very angry, and he did not wish to be so. He said, "I think we'd better stop talking and save our strength."

"For that matter," she said, "what sense is there in two resurrections or in having a millennium? Why lock up Satan for a thousand years and then release him to lead the heathens against the Christians again, only to lock him up again and then hold the final judgment?"

He did not answer, and she said nothing more for a long time. After an hour, they came down out of the jumbled and shattered hills, and Kelvin saw the white horse eating some long brown grass growing from between tiny cracks in the rocks. They approached slowly while Kelvin called out softly to him. The animal trotted off, however, when Kelvin was only forty feet away from him. He aimed his rifle at it; he could not let this much meat get away now on the slim chance that he might catch it later on.

Dana Webster said, "Don't shoot it! I'll get him!" She called out loudly. The horse wheeled, snorting, and ran up to her and nuzzled her. She patted it and smiled at Kelvin. "I have a feeling for animals," she said. "Rather, there's a good feeling between me and them. An ESP of some sort, sympathetic vibrations, call it what you will."

"Beauty and the beast."

She quit smiling. "The Beast?"

"I didn't mean that. But your power over animals. . . ."

"Don't tell me you believe in witchcraft? Good God! And I'm not swearing when I say that. Don't you believe in love? He feels it. And I feel such a traitor getting him back, because he'll probably be eaten."

An hour later, they led the horse, worn-out from carrying the two humans, into camp near the sea. The sentinels had challenged them, and Kelvin had given the proper countersigns. They passed them and entered a depression on a jagged but low hill. All around them was the mouth-watering odor of frying fish. The four men who had put out into the red-tinged waters in the small, lightweight, collapsible boat had been fortunate. Or blessed by God. They had not expected to catch anything at all, because the fish-life had been frighteningly depleted. When St. John had predicted that a third of the seas would be destroyed, he had underestimated. Rather, underpredicted.

Dana Webster pointed at the thirteen large fish frying in the dural pans over the firs. She said. "Does that mean we won't have to slaughter the horse?"

"Not now, anyway," he said.

"I'm so glad."

Kelvin was glad, too, but he was not impressed by her love for it. He had known too many butchers of children who were very much concerned about humane treatment for dogs and cats.

The men and women waiting for them were lean and dark with the sun and wind and were ridged, as if they were pieces of mahogany carved by windblown sand. They shone with something of a great strength derived from certainty. They had been through the persecutions and the cataclysms and the battles against the slaves of the Beast after the Beast's power had been broken by the cataclysms. "Blessed and holy is he who shares in the first resurrection! Over such the second death has no power, but they shall be priests of God and of Christ and they shall reign with him a thousand years."

However, Kelvin thought, the statement that the second death will have no power over them apparently meant that those who had resisted the Beast for love of God would not be judged again. But they *could* die, and those who died would not return to the Earth until the thousand years had passed. And then they would rise with the other dead in their new bodies and witness the final judgment. It was then that those faithful who had died before the time of the Beast would be given new bodies and the others would go to whatever fate awaited them. The Alpha and Omega, the final kingdom, would come.

All this had gone into the shaping of their bodies and the expression of face and eye. They were saints now, and nothing could ever change that. But saints could go hungry and thirsty and get very tired and become discouraged. And they would kill if they must.

There were no children here nor had any of the party seen anyone under seven during their journey across the continent and the seas. Their time would come at the end of the millennium.

"What do we have here?" Anna Silvich said.

Anna was a tall gray-eyed blonde who would have been beautiful under softer conditions. Now her flesh was pared away so that the bones seemed very near and the white skin was dark and cracked. Despite this, Kelvin had felt very attracted to her. He intended to ask her to be his wife after they reached the beloved city. He could have married her before this, if she would have him, since any of the party could conduct the ceremony. They were all priests now. But he did not want to do anything that would take his mind off the most important object: getting to the beloved city.

"We have here one who claims she is a Christian," Kelvin said.

Anna took a pencil-shaped plastic object from her shirt-pocket, pointed it at Dana Webster's forehead, and slid a section of the object forward.

"See?" Webster said. "I don't have the mark of the Beast."

Anna stepped forward and seized the woman's hair and pulled her head down. Kelvin started to protest against the unnecessary roughness, but he decided not to. He would see how Webster reacted; perhaps she might get angry enough to trip herself up. Anna released the woman's hair and said, "No scars there. But that doesn't mean anything. If I had a microscope or even a magnifying glass. . . ."

Dana Webster said nothing but looked scornful. If she were upset or angry about her treatment, however, she did not allow it to interfere with her appetite. She ate the fish and the biscuits and canned peaches. The latter two items had been found in the ruins of a house by Sherborn, a little man who had a nose for buried or concealed food.

Kelvin had given the prayer of thankfulness before they ate, but he felt he should say more afterwards. "God has been good and given us enough today to restore our strength. We can face tomorrow with the certain knowledge that He will provide more. It's evident from today's catch that there are still fish in the Mediterranean. There must be enough to keep us fed until we get to the beloved city."

Dana Webster, he noticed, said amen to that just as the others did. That could mean nothing except that she was playing her role of Christian, if she was indeed playing. She could be sincere. On the other hand, there were her remarks while they were traveling campwards. He asked her what she had meant by *Extraterrestrials*.

She looked around at the dark faces with their protruding cheekbones and hollow cheeks and the darkly rimmed but fire-bright eyes. "I should have kept these doubts—or, rather, speculations—to myself," she said. "I should've waited until we got to the beloved city. Then everything would be straightened out. One way or another. Of course, by then it might be too late for us. I hate to say anything about this because you'll think I'm a heathen. But I have a mind, and I must speak it. Isn't that the Christian way?"

"We're not slaves of the Beast, if that's what you mean," Anna said. "We won't kill somebody because they differ somewhat from us on certain theological matters. Of course, we won't listen to blasphemy. But then you won't blaspheme if you're a Christian."

"It's easy to see you don't like me, Anna Silvich," Webster said. "Of course, that doesn't mean you're not a Christian. You can love mankind but dislike a particular person for one or another reason. Even if she is a fellow believer. Still, that doesn't mean that you're excused from examining yourself and finding out why you can't love me."

Anna said, with only a slight quaver of anger, "Yes, I don't like you. There is something about you . . . some . . . odor. . . ."

"Of brimstone, I suppose?" Dana Webster said.

"God forgive me if I'm wrong," Anna said. "But you know what we've all been through. The betrayals, the spies, the prisons, seeing our children and mates tortured and then beheaded, our supposed friends turning their backs on us or turning us in, the terrible, terrible things done to us. But you know this, whether you're what you say you are or a Judas. However, you are right in reproaching me for one thing. I shouldn't say you stink of the devil unless I really have proof. But. . . ."

"But you have said so and therefore you've stained me in everybody's thoughts," Dana said. "Couldn't you have waited until you were certain, instead of maliciously, and most unchristianly stigmatizing me?"

"Somehow, we've strayed from the original question," Kelvin said. "What do you mean, Dana, by *Extraterrestrials?*"

She looked around at the faces in the firelight and then at the shadows outside as if there were things in the shadows. "I know you won't even want to consider what I'm going to speculate about. You're too tired in body and mind, too numb with the horrors of the persecution and the cataclysms and the battles that followed, to think about one more battle, or series of battles. But do I have to remind you that men have been looking for the apocalypse for two thousand years? And that there have been many times when men claimed that it was not only at hand but had actually begun?

"There have been times when men who spoke with authority, or seeming authority, proclaimed that the end of the world was at hand.

Seabury-Western Seminary Library
2122 She
Evanston.

But they were all mistaken, deceived by themselves or by the Enemy. Which may be the same. I mean, the Enemy may be the enemy within ourselves, not an entity, a unique person with an objective existence outside of us. The point is, what if we're being fooled again? Not self-deceived, as in the past, but deceived by an outside agency? By Extraterrestrials who are using weapons against Earth, weapons which far surpass ours? And now we're being asked to gather at the so-called beloved city, asked to come in and surrender. Why? Perhaps we're to form the basis of the future slave population for these beings?"

There was a long silence afterwards. Anna Silvich broke it by crying, "You have convicted yourself, woman! You are trying to put doubts into our hearts, to destroy our faith! You are a heathen!"

Kelvin held his hands up for silence, and, when that did not work, shouted at Anna and the others to shut up. When the uproar had died, he said, "What evidence do you have that your Extraterrestrials exist, Dana?"

"Exactly the same evidence you have that this is the beginning of the millennium," she said. "The difference is my interpretation. Try to look at the situation, and our theories, objectively. And remember that the Antichrist fooled many, probably including some right here, when he claimed to be Christ. He has been exposed and, supposedly, defeated for all time. Or, at least until the final battle a thousand years from now. But think. Could it be Satan himself who was trying his final trick on us? Or could it be that Extraterrestrials who knew of the longing of the faithful for the millennium have caused this pseudomillennium to occur? And. . . ."

"Or perhaps it is Satan who is using the Extraterrestrials?" Anna said scornfully.

"It could be," Dana Webster said.

"Just a minute," Kelvin said. "I can't for the life of me, the soul of me, I should say, imagine why these Extraterrestrials should bring the faithful back to life? What reason could they have to do that?"

"Have you seen any of the resurrected?" Dana Webster said. "Is there anybody in this group who has seen one of them? Or, perhaps, some among you were killed and then brought back to life?"

Kelvin said, "It's true that no one here was restored to life. But it is not true that none of us have seen a resurrected person. I myself talked with a man who had been killed for his faith, though he was given the chance to deny God and become a slave of the Beast after seeing his wife and children raped and tortured and then beheaded. But he refused and so he was roasted over the fire and his head cut off. But he awoke at the bottom of the grave which had been opened for him, and he crawled out and was with a number of others who had been brought back to life. His wife and children were not among them, but he was sure that he would find them. I had no reason to doubt him, since I had known him from childhood."

"What do you think of that, Webster?" Anna said.

"But you did not see him killed, nor did you see him resurrected, isn't that right?" Webster said. "How do you know that he did not in actuality deny God and become a slave of the Beast? How do you know that his story about his resurrection was not a lie, that he wasn't lying so he could pass himself off as a Christian, since he had fallen among Christians? Indeed, it would be wise of the Enemy, whether Satan or Extraterrestrial, to send out spies with these lying stories so they could deceive the Christians."

Kelvin had to admit to himself that he had no proof of his friend's story and that what Webster postulated could be true. But he did not think that she was right. Some things had to be taken on faith. On the other hand, the Antichrist had fooled many, including himself at first. He gestured impatiently and said, "All this talk! We'll take you with us to the city, and when we get there, we'll find out the truth about everything."

"Why take her along?" Anna said. "She's convicted herself out of her own mouth with her lies, and she'll be an extra mouth to feed. . . ."

"Anna!" Kelvin said. "That's not loving. . . ."

"The time has come and gone for loving your enemies!" Anna said. "The new times are here; there is no room for tolerance of heathens. And we can't take her along, because she'll be lying to us with her tales of Extraterrestials and other subtleties designed to make us fall into error! And we haven't anyone to ask what we should do with her. We have to make up our own minds and act on our decision, hard though it may seem."

Dana Webster gave a little start. Even by the firelight, she could be seen to pale. She pointed past Anna and said, quietly but with a tremor in her voice, "Why don't you ask him what to do?"

They spun around, their hands going for their weapons. But the tall man in white robes and with short hair as white as newly-washed wool had his hands high up in the air so they could see he was unarmed. He was smiling; his teeth were very white in the firelight, and his eyes were shining with the reflected light. The eyes of no human being shone like those; they were like a lion's. Nor could any human being have crept by the sentinels and appeared so suddenly. The breeze, which Kelvin had suddenly felt just before Webster had spoken, must have been the air displaced by the emergence of this man . . . person . . . from nowhere. Kelvin felt his skin grow cold over his scalp and the back of his neck. He was scared, yet he was glad. At least, someone to tell them what was happening and what they must do, had come.

The man slowly lowered his hands. He was very handsome and very clean and had a beautiful well-proportioned body, quite in contrast to the ragged, dirty, scruffy bunch, scarred and skinny and stinking. The man slowly opened his robes so that they could see that he had no concealed weapons beneath them. They could also see that he was sexless. And, now that Kelvin was coming out of the shock of the sudden appearance, he saw that *he* was a misnomer. The being's features were effeminate. But the total impression the being gave was more masculine than feminine, and so Kelvin continued to think of the person as he.

He said, "You may call me Jones. I'll take up only a few minutes of your time."

Kelvin recognized the deep rich voice. It was the same voice that came to them from time to time, over their transistor receivers. It was the voice that had told the faithful all over the world to start out for the beloved city. It had also told a little about what was expected from the faithful when they did get to the beloved city. Only one thing was clear. The new citizens would have much hard work to do for a long, long time.

"We would be honored, and very happy, if you would stay for more than a few minutes . . . Mr. Jones," Kelvin said. "We have many questions. We also have a crucial problem here."

The angel looked at Dana Webster, but he did not lose his smile. "I don't know what your problem is with her, but I'm sure you'll do the right thing," he said. "As for your questions, most of them will have to wait. I'm busy just now. We have a thousand years to get ready for, and that will pass quickly enough for those who will live through it."

It was difficult to get up enough courage to argue with an angel, but Kelvin had not survived because of lack of courage. He said, "Why do we have to get to the beloved city on our own? We've suffered enough, I would think, and several of our party have been killed by heathens or in accidents. That doesn't seem to jibe with what we read in St. John the Divine. . . ."

Jones raised a long slim hand on the back of which were many white woolly hairs. He said, still smiling, "I don't know the answer to that, any more than I know why there is a first death and then a second death or why all the heathens weren't killed or why they will flourish and propagate once more. Some of whom, by the way, will be your children and grandchildren to the 250th generation, to your sorrow, though not to your everlasting sorrow. Don't ask me why. I know more than you, but I don't know everything. I am content to wait until the obscurities and ambiguities and seeming paradoxes are straightened out. And you will have to wait. Unless you are killed, of course, and spared the thousand years of struggle."

"We are as subject as ever to the whims of chance!" Kelvin said. "I thought. . . ."

"You thought you'd have everything programmed, everything certain and easy," Jones said. "Well, God has always dealt with this world on a statistical basis, excepting certain people and events. And, generally speaking, He will continue to do so until the second death. Then, my friend, He will deal with every bit of matter in this world, and the souls that inhabit certain material forms, on a specific and individual basis. And that will be the difference between the world as it has been, and the new, unfluctuating, and unchanging world as it will be after the second death. Not that He is not aware of every atom now and what it is doing. But in the unchanging time to come, He will have His hand upon all matter and all souls, and nothing will evolve or change. You might say that, up to now, and until the thousand years are over, He has respected Heisenberg's principle of uncertainty." Jones looked at each intently, still smiling, and then said, "Actually, I'm here in my office—one of many—of requisitioner. I'm taking your horse, which is needed at the city."

"Why don't you just create some horses and leave this one with us?" Anna said. "We need it for food."

"There's other food to be had," Jones said. "This horse is destined to be the father of many hundreds of thousands. As far as I know, the only new creations will be after the second death, when you fortunate ones will be given new bodies. Something like the one I'm using."

That answered one question. There would be no sex in the new earth and the new heaven. And why should there be? There would be no more babies, and the ecstasy of beholding God's face would far transcend any fleshly delights. Despite this, Kelvin felt a panic. He would be castrated. Then he told himself that he would have to get over that reaction. There would be compensations which would make the loss of his sex seem trivial and, perhaps, a cause for rejoicing. Nor would he be any less a man, that is, a human being.

Anna said, loudly, "There is one thing you should know so you can report it to your superiors, even if you won't do anything about it here!"

Jones raised his woolly white eyebrows and said, "Superiors? I have only two, and I won't have to report to them. They know what's going on at every second."

Anna was checked, but she rallied after a moment's silence. She said, "Forgive me if I'm presuming. But you should know that this woman here claims that all this, that is, the events of the past four years, have been caused by Extraterrestrials! She says we're being fooled! It's all a trick of things from outer space or wherever they come from! What do you say to that?"

Jones smiled and said, "Well, angels *are* Extraterrestrial beings, though not all Extraterrestrials are angels. As I said, it's your problem. You're grown up now, though still, of course, children of God. I go now. God bless you." Jones mounted the horse and rode out of sight down a defile. Kelvin climbed up onto the shoulder of a high hill to watch him ride out. He heard the bang, like a large balloon exploding, as the air rushed in to fill the vacuum left by a suddenly unoccupied space.

After five minutes, he climbed back down.

"If he wanted the horse, why didn't he just take it?" Anna said.

"Surely he could have done it without leaving the city."

"Perhaps teleportation requires that the teleporter has to be physically present to do the work." Dana said.

"Teleportation?" Anna said. "That was an angel, you fool. Angels don't have to resort to teleportation."

"Teleportation is only a term used to describe a phenomenon," Dana said. "It's the same whether it's brought about by an angel or an Extraterrestrial."

"And you're a heathen," Anna said. "That angel must think we're a fine bunch of featherbrains if we can't see what's so obvious. He was laughing at us because we were so stupid."

"He could have been laughing because I told you the truth and you wouldn't believe it," Dana Webster said.

"And if he was one of your creatures from outer space, why didn't he just wipe us out," Anna said, "or just teleport us to the city? It would be so easy for him."

"I don't know," Dana Webster said. "Maybe they're giving us some sort of test so they can decide where to assign us for some sort of job. Those who survive the terrible journey to the city get some sort of booby prize. Or become the studs and mares of a new breed of superslaves. I don't know."

The effect of her words was stronger than Kelvin liked. Too many looked as if they were seriously considering her speculations.

It rained heavily that night, as it had for almost every night for three years. Everybody was soaked, but no one came down with colds or pneumonia or any respiratory disease. Yet, many had been subject to colds and allergic to pollen or suffering from various degrees of emphysema before the cataclysms had begun. Something had rid them of all diseases, in fact, and Kelvin pointed this out that morning. He indicated it as evidence that they would all be free of body infirmities and ailments, and would not age for a thousand years. Yet microorganisms continued to do their work on dead bodies. Meat got spoiled; dead animals, and humans, rotted. Surely, this discrimination was God-given. Why should the Enemy, or Extraterrestrials, give human beings immunity from disease?

"I don't know," Dana Webster said. "We'll find out. Also, have the heathens been given this same immunity? If they have, then surely God is not responsible for the immunity, that is, He is not responsible for the dispensation of immunity. He, of course, is primarily responsible for anything that happens, in that it can't happen unless He permits it."

Kelvin expected her to bring up the question of why a good God would permit evil in the first place, but she did not push that time-waster on them.

The days and nights, the burning under the sun and the cold soaking at night, went on and on. A thousand miles of desert along the sea behind them and another thousand to go.

Dana Webster had more than done her share. She was a genius at catching lizards and finding large quantities of locusts and stunning birds and the little desert foxes with her slings. The items she brought to the community pot were not attractive, but they were nutritious and filled the belly. Even Anna had to admit that the party had eaten better since Webster joined them. But Anna also pointed out that Webster's very gift at hunting could be due to a strange power she had over animals. And who knew but that this was because she was herself one of the slaves of the Beast. Ex-slaves rather, since the Beast was now in the lake of burning brimstone. But the ex-slaves were still dedicated to evil, of course.

Kelvin had become irritated at Dana Webster's attitude, since he was now very attracted to her. In fact, he told himself during a fit of honesty, he was in love with her. He did not tell Dana, of course, because he could never marry her if she were a heathen. There had been a time when Christians had married heathens, but that must never be again. There was no doubt any more about the line between good and evil. That is, as far as marriage went, there was no doubt about the lines. But there was still doubt about the honesty and the motives of people. And he was not sure what Dana Webster was. Sometimes, she talked so close to blasphemy that he felt repelled. Or uneasy. And he was uneasy because she seemed to be making some sense. At other times, he thought that she was truly a Christian but one who did not trust appearances and so was perhaps oversuspicious. But, in this world of untrustworthy appearances, could a person be overly suspicious?

Whatever the truth, he now yearned for this woman as he had

yearned for none, not even Anna, since his wife had betrayed him. Was there something still evil in him, something that attracted him to women who had enlisted for Satan? But he had been attracted to Anna, and surely she was not on the Enemy's side? Nor did he have any proof that Dana was with the Enemy.

It did not seem likely that some residue of evil still lay deep within him. He had refused to go along with the Beast, and he had survived the cataclysms and the overthrow of the Beast, and so the second death had no power over him. He had been judged once and for all.

But could it be that he still needed refining, that there were elements of evil in him, and that the thousand years were to be used to purge him? Was that why the millennium must be? So that the surviving Christians could be purged of all evil? What, then, would purge those who had died and who would arise at the second judgment and be given new bodies? Why did they not have to go through the fire of a thousand years?

One night, Dana, who had been silent about her theories of the reality of the situation for a long time, proposed a new theory. "Those prophets who come closest to predicting the future as it really develops are those whose minds have an inborn computer. They don't truly prophesy, in the sense that they can actually look into the future. No, their minds, unconsciously, of course, compute the highest probabilities, and it is the most likely course of events that they predict. Or choose, rather. Your true prophet has a gift which is not a clairvoyance but is the selection of what is most probable. He sees the *in potentio* as actualized, though vaguely and in large general terms. His vision must necessarily be cast into symbolic images because he can't understand what he sees. He can't because he is a creature of the present, and the future contains many unfamiliar things."

"But John saw what was revealed by God," Anna said. "God would not reveal a probability; He would show only a certainty."

Dana shrugged and said, "Sometimes, a prophet will get two probable futures mixed up. He'll not be able to differentiate between the most likely and the next most likely. He sees the future as one, but in reality he is witnessing a part of one probable future inserted in the continuum of another probable future. That is why, perhaps, John saw two resurrections, the millennium, and so forth. He saw two or more futures all mixed up. Only true events will straighten out what future is really the most probable. Do you follow me?"

"And I suppose he may have seen Extraterrestrials and thought they were angels?" Anna said.

"It's possible."

Anna stood up and cried, "She is saying all these confusing things to lead us astray!"

"But you can't be led astray," Dana Webster said. "Only the heathen can now be led astray."

"Not if your theory is right," Anna said, and then she stared at Webster in an obvious confusion.

The entire party was upset. The next night, seeing that the situation had not improved, even though Dana had refused to talk about her theories any more, Kelvin held a conference. After he had Dana taken to one side, he said to the others, "We may be saints, but we're certainly not behaving as such. Now, I've heard some of you, especially Anna, say that Dana should be killed. You don't even want just to kick her out of our party, because she might then find some heathens and lead them to attack us. Or because she may be the mother of heathens, and such should not be allowed to breed.

"Anna, would you be the one to shoot her in cold blood if we decided that she should die?"

"It wouldn't be in cold blood!" Anna said.

"Would it be in hate then? With an unchristian desire to shed blood?"

"At one time," Anna said, "it would have been a sin to hate. But the first death has come, and the old order has passed away, and the new one has come. There is no more returning of lost sheep to the fold. Once a heathen, always a heathen. That is the way it is now."

"The old order will not pass away until after the second death," Kelvin said. "I quote you Revelation 21:4: 'Now God's home is with men! He will live with them and they shall be his people. God Himself will be with them. . . . He will wipe away all tears from their eyes. There will be no more death, no more grief, crying, or pain. The old things have disappeared.' And don't forget what John says in 20:13, '. . . and all were judged according to what they had done.' If we kill Dana Webster, we will be judged by what we have done, which will be, in my opinion, murder."

"But you said we won't be judged again!" Anna said. "And remember what that angel said. Whatever we do, it will be the right thing!"

Kelvin was silent for a while. Everything was so tangled and shadowy, not bright and straight as it was supposed to be after the Beast had been put away. Or had they misunderstood the real meaning of the Revelation? What was it supposed to be? John had not said so or even implied it. Kelvin, like so many, had just assumed it.

It was then that Anna said that they would all starve if Dana Webster had to be fed, and that she should be killed before she could say another word of her blasphemous speculations.

"We have eaten better since Dana joined us," Kelvin said. "You know that to be true, Anna, so why do you lie? Listen, all of you, whatever else is not clear in this hot and dusty world, two things are. It is by these two that we must live, and by these two that we must die. One is, love God. The other is, love your fellow man. As long as Dana claims to be a Christian, then we must treat her as one until we get proof to the contrary."

"Many of us were delivered into the hands of the torturer and the butcher because of that," Anna said.

"So be it," Kelvin said. "But that is the way it must be. We take her along to the beloved city, and when we're there, then we'll find out."

Anna walked away. Others were not happy about his decision but, in these hard and dangerous times, there was no room for committee action. Like it or not, survival depended upon the quick rule of one good man.

Dana, smiling, though still pale, came up to him and kissed him on the lips. Kelvin felt a spasm of desire for her, but he pushed her away, though gently. He could not marry her now, or perhaps, ever. Not until they got to the city would he find out what was or was not permitted. And if he allowed his desire to overrule his good sense and he married her now, the group would believe, perhaps rightly, that he had put his self above the good of the whole.

Nevertheless, he did not get to sleep easily that night, and he found himself straining through the darkness towards Dana, as if his soul itself were trying to lift his body up and propel it through the air to her. The rains fell, and he huddled under the shelf of rock and wished he had her warm body inside the blanket with him. After a while, he prayed himself to sleep.

He awoke to shouting, screams, curses, the sound of the edge of steel striking flesh, and the shots from those of his party who had awakened in time.

Kelvin got off one shot, saw the dark figure before him fall, and something struck his head. He awoke shortly after dawn with a headache like a hot stone in his brain. His hands were tied behind him, and his feet were hobbled. Six of the attackers, all in ragged black and gold uniforms of the soldiers of the Beast, were standing over the survivors of his party. Little Jessica Crenwell lay on her back, unconscious and groaning, and apparantly not long for life. Dana Webster rose from beside Crenwell and walked towards him. She seemed unhurt. And she carried a rifle.

He suppressed a groan and said, "So Anna was right "

But she was not, as he had expected, pleased.

"I had nothing to do with these," she said, gesturing at the sullen-faced heathen. "At least, I did not tell them to attack. They have ruined my plans to enter your beloved city with your party. Now I'll have to find another party of fools or somehow manage to convince the city's guardians that I am what I claim to be. And that won't be easy."

"I don't understand," he said, wincing from the pain involved in talking. "If you meant to palm yourself off as a Christian, why did you argue so vehemently that this was a false apocalypse? Why your theory of the Extraterrestrials?"

She smiled then, and she said, "Long before we reached the city, I would have pretended to have converted wholly to your way of thinking. I would have repented my errors. You would then accept me far more easily, because I would have seemed to have been confused and hurt by my traumatic experiences but would have been cured, shown the right way. And then you wouldn't have had much hesitation about marrying me, would you?"

"To be honest, no. I would have rejoiced at your change and leaped at the chance to marry you. But I would have done so only if you had made it plain that you really wanted me."

"And I would have arranged it so that you would not have been able to hold out," she said. "And then, as your wife, as one of the faithful band, I would have started planting my little seeds of doubt here and there, watering them on the sly, and all the time determining the weaknesses and the strengths of the city for the day when we attack."

"We?"

"We have been chosen by the new rulers of Earth as the favored executives, the herders of the swine. We were approached before all this began, told what would happen, and given our duties. And it was all as they said it would be. They are your true prophets, my friend, not some old half-crazy man on an island. They knew that the stresses inside the Earth would bring on the greatest quakes the Earth has ever known, and they knew that a group of large asteroids was heading for the Earth. Why shouldn't they, since they launched the asteroids ages ago, and since they have devices to store up energy in the Earth and to trigger it off whenever they care to do so."

"They?" Kelvin said, and he felt the stone in his brain become bigger and hotter.

"They are from a planet which orbits a star in Andromeda. They are the true rulers of this universe, or destined to be such. They can travel through interstellar space at speeds far exceeding those of light. But there is another race which has the same powers, and an evil race which has been the eon-long enemy of the Andromedans."

Kelvin groaned, partly from the agony in his head and partly from the agony in his soul.

"Your story sounds vaguely familiar," he said. "And I'm not referring to the science-fiction stories we used to read before the Beast suppressed them."

"It's in the Bible," she said, "but in a rather distorted form. I wasn't lying when I said that some men could compute the most probable future. To some extent, that is, on a broad and unspecific scale, of course. However, the Arcturans were going to seize Earth and take over when the Andromedans struck. The Arcturans are those you think of as angels. They are the ones preparing to build the beloved city, which will be a fortress to hold Earth—they think."

Kelvin said, "Satan may be locked up, but surely his aides are loose. But they won't be able to do anything really drastic for a long, long time. Not for a thousand years."

She laughed and said, "You still insist on believing your old cast-off myth?"

"It is you who believe in the myth, though it is new," he said. "You have to rationalize. You have to believe that the evil spirits are not spirits but beings from another star. And they, of course, must be the good ones, because no one really allies himself with what he admits is an evil cause. No, somehow, the cause must be a good one, no matter what evil it does. And we Christians, of course, are the evil ones. The Enemy has to think of himself as good."

The other heathens were walking towards him. They held knives and cigarette lighters.

Dana Webster said, "I must go now. I have work to do. I leave you to these. They'd be angry if I frustrated them by killing you. I need them, so they'll get their way now. I'm sorry, in a way, since I don't like torture. But there are times when it must be used."

"That's the difference between me and you, between us and your kind," Kelvin said. "I pity you, Dana Webster, I pity you from the deepest part of my being. I wish even now that you could see the light, that you could love God, know God as I know Him. But it is too late. The thousand years have started, and your end is foretold.

"And if I scream, *when* I scream, I should say, and if I beg for mercy from these things that have no mercy, and if I scream at them to get it over with —well, no matter how long it seems, it will be over. And then I will arise in a new body, and the old order will have passed away, and there will be no death any longer or any grief or pain."

"You nauseating egotistic fool!" she said.

"Time will tell which of us is a fool," he said. "But time has already told which of us is for man and God."

As death came, a smile passed, fleetingly, over his face—a smile Dana Webster would not, indeed, could not understand.

chronicles of a comer

BY K. M. O'DONNELL

SEPTEMBER 14: Harder and harder to concentrate upon the demographic urges of Dayton, Ohio, that most American of the American cities. Fourteen percent of college-educated housewives believe in stronger repressive measures against the drug-culture; fifty-one percent of working-class males above the median in salary believe that television is a government plot. Etc. Sitting here, the figures heaped before me, graphing them out slowly and neatly into the presentation brochures, I feel a sense of uselessness overcoming me unlike any I have ever known . . . and I have often felt useless. What does it matter? Who cares? What would the working class of males say to my condition? I believe in the Second Coming.

I believe in the Second Coming. Putting down this sentence in the journal of my thoughts and activities I have just decided to keep, I feel a thrill of sheer madness going through me; a throbbing unleashed that causes me to literally shift in place, cover this entry apprehensively lest a strolling Supervisor wander through to peer down at my work and see what has been written. *I believe in the Second Coming.* Perhaps I should seek psychiatric help which is at least partially covered by the company benefit program. Nevertheless I do. Indications point to it. Breakdown, dislocation, strange noises and rising from the East; assassination, great alienation and discontent, the scar of barbarism opening up deep within the layers of the culture. Conditions force. According to the most informed readings of the Book of Daniel it will occur within the next ten years; then again, according to other discredited authorities, it might have happened in 1928. No matter, no matter. It will happen. A small pulse of necessity flowers within me, guiding my hand through this entry and as if from a far distance I hear the bell of Apocalypse striking.

I wonder what form He will take so that, as promised, all witnessing will know Him.

September 15: Failure with Francine again tonight. Our marriage has arced downward, a clear bell curve of declension in recent months, now . . . I can no longer bear to touch her. Preoccupied with the larger considerations of last judgement . . . I cannot concentrate upon her any more; . . . cannot even take our troubles seriously. "You don't care," she says, "you don't care about people. You're just a cold-hearted statistician who sees people as numbers and trends. You fooled me for a while but that's all you ever were. You do not care."

She is right but she is wrong. I do not care about people (because they will merely bear witness to the Coming) but I am not a cold-hearted statistician. More and more, the devices of my work seem insane to me: what does Kettering or Dayton, Ohio, have to do with the high, pure cleaning flame, the clean arching notes of the trumpet signalling time come around again? It is hard to believe that I ever took this seriously. That I ever took Francine seriously. Tonight I tried, however.

I took her to dinner, listened to her little complaints and held my peace for the evening, brought her back to the apartment and finally tried to make love. How long, how long it had truly been since I felt desire! But the fleeting desire quickly perished, my mind scurrying off into a small abscess where I saw and heard the form that the last judgment would take and where our pitiful little struggles would stand against the bar of Heaven.

Passion ebbed quickly and a sense of revulsion overcame me. Behind me she said things which I would not hear. I have failed with her before but never for reasons so justified and now I am in a high, cold place where she cannot touch me. I do not care whether she leaves or not.

September 16: At lunch hour today, a quick walk on Lexington Avenue to restore the circulation, brush thoughts of Dayton machinists and schoolchildren from my mind. In the doorways prostitutes, beggars, and obscurely displaced of the city whom I once fantasized kept the machinery going through the principles of necessary inefficiency. "Give me some money, you," a particularly vicious beggar said to me as I stepped out across Twenty-fourth Street, "who do you think you are?"

The impulse for flight quickly cancelled, I turned upon the beggar ready for confrontation . . . and then it occurred to me in a great burst of light that there was no saying what form He will take upon His ascension; He is as likely to be a beggar as to return in more glorious forms. Quickly, I searched the creature's face for indications of sacrament but could detect nothing but loathing and aggression. Still, how are we to know? Can we judge at this plane the devices of the saints? "Are you . . ." I started to say and then balked to an embarrassed muteness. I realized that I was about to ask the beggar if he were the Saviour.

"My God," he said, "I think you're crazy," and sprinted from me quickly, turning a corner and being gone. In the distance I heard an explosion which might have been the backfire of a bus or the sound of the beggar reassuming his natural form and going to a High Place. Who can tell? What is there to know? I continued meditating on my way, unable to escape the exciting feeling which has come over me since I started this journal. I am in the midst of climactic events.

September 17: Nothing happened today. Air thick, oppressive, damping down upon the city; news of the shooting of yet another Presidential candidate. Indications accelerate. Francine left me today. She was not at the apartment when I returned. She had removed her clothing and I discarded her note without reading.

September 18: Problems at the company. Called into the supervisor's office this morning; told that my work had been falling off seriously in recent weeks. Simple statistical errors, flaws of computation a child would not have made, misplacement of median and mode. "We cannot tolerate this kind of thing," the supervisor went on to say (am omitting proper names from this journal as much as possible; Francine's only mentioned because she has no effect upon my life), "precision, grace, close tolerances, market research, dependent advertisers, key demographics," and so on, and with a final admonition sent me from his office with the clear indication that career and salary plan or not, my position may be considered somewhat endangered at the present time.

What would it benefit him if I told the basis for my distraction, outlined my conviction that very little can be taken seriously at the present moment since time itself is ending? He would not understand and my job would be further endangered,and then again, more terrifyingly, he might understand perfectly and his bland, blank eyes would focus upon me in perfect stillness and peace, all of his features rotating toward waxy flexibility. "Just tell me how soon," he would say then in a little voice, "that's all I want to know. How soon because really, I too cannot take this any more."

September 19: At lunch hour I think I saw the beggar again but then I am not sure; he fled so quickly when our paths intersected on the sidewalk. "What's wrong with you?" a voice said to me while I was walking abstractedly; "anyway, give me all your money," but as I turned to the sound he must have recognized me and whisked away. Maybe. Perhaps. It does not explain the source of his terror (unless any knowledge of his true identity would shift the Plans) nor does it bring me any closer to a pinpointing of the date when he may be expected to shed his earthly mask and appear before us in His true substance.

Utterly missed a distribution curve today and had to redo an entire chart. I agree. My work is not what it once was.

September 20: The wounded Presidential candidate may recover. Then again he may not. It is difficult to make a medical judgment at this time; fortunately he is a minor party candidate . . . so the true course of the election has not been affected. Candidates from the major parties have reduced their speaking schedules to closed auditoriums and security has been tightened even further. Two Eastern nations, through the proxies of their Heads of State, have declared a final war. The President, himself not a candidate for re-election, has appeared on television urging calm. In Dayton the appeal has been met with apparent calm. The indications quicken; the world is a great artery being brought to the knife.

Francine reappeared. "I thought you would worry," she said, "I thought you would try to find me. I thought you would read my note and understand that I only left you out of desperation and wanted to shock you into understanding. But now I realize that I was wrong all the time and that there is nothing there. This is the last time. I am coming only to pick up my last things; my lawyer will hear of this and he will be in touch with you. Do not speak to me. You didn't even read my note, did you?"

There is nothing to say to her. I have nothing to say to her. While she bangs around the apartment, muttering, I sit in a corner of the living room, in a chair, and read the newspapers carrying further reports of the wondrous signs and portents. It occurs to me that perhaps I should check her out more carefully, at least to see if there is any possibility that He is made manifest in her . . . but that is clearly impossible. This at least I know if I know nothing else: He would not return to earth in the form of a woman.

September 21: Forty-three percent of central America disapproves of the shooting of even minor candidates for President, tentative conclusion. Disapproval is highest among college graduates, lower . . . as expected . . . in those with only a high school education. There is a coefficient of correlation of .85 between approval of the shooting of bizarre candidates and a belief in the immorality of pre-marital sexual intercourse. I do not know what to make of this nor are my speculations needed. I convey the figures, the charts, the random patterning, the tentative graphs to my supervisor who looks at them quizzically and says that they will have to be forwarded on for further processing.

At lunch hour I look for the beggar who has become an important part of my life but do not see him. Perhaps He is already at this moment in seclusion, preparing His garments for the Ascension and no longer walking to and fro in the Earth or upon it as He prepares for His enormous tasks.

September 22: He will come wearing a crown of fire, He will come from the high place and stand above us, He will bring down His hand and signal the beginning of the one thousand years of destruction which must precede His eternal reign, but even knowing this, I am calm; time has come around again, we can no longer tolerate what has become of us. My belief has become my armor; in its coolness I dwell, acceptance of the spirit, no trembling of the flesh, and when He brings down His hand then to start the fires I will stand among the steadfast, calm in the righteousness of my vision, protected by the depth of my acceptance.

One of the wounded candidates passed into a coma this morning and is not expected to recover. Bombs are falling upon the nations of the East and no quick conclusion to the war is expected. In the mails this morning arrived a letter from a man representing himself to be Francine's lawyer, asking for a full accounting of my position. I wish, I only wish that I could share it with him.

September 23: Dayton, Ohio, reacts, according to the first quick surveys, with great calm to the death of the unfortunate Presidential candidate. The coefficient of correlation between acceptance of his death and the belief in a really effective headache remedey appears to be upwards of .75. These conclusions will be telephoned immediately to our client, the headache remedy company. "It's a crazy business," my superior says (he has moments of recrimination), shaking his head, and I do not have the heart to tell him that soon his business, along with everything else, will be no more. Like so many of us, like the way I used to, he holds onto the devices of his life as if they were imperishable artifacts bridging or containing all reality; I would not take this away from him. In time he too will accept the judgment. For now he contents himself with verifying and transmitting the tentative conclusions as . . . locked to my desk . . . I work my pencil through the forms and look out the window occasionally, waiting for the first glimpse of that rosy haze which, I know, will signal culmination.

September 24:

September 25:

September 26: Still too weak to write today. Maybe tomorrow. Oh my God.

September 27: I did nothing; he fell upon me like a beast . . . and oh my Lord my body is a wound. Tomorrow. Tomorrow I will be better. I will write more tomorrow. At least I did not have to be hospitalized . . . although the company would have covered everything.

September 28: Stronger, but inside broken. The end of the weekend which coincided with the attack . . . so at least I did not miss more than three days of work. Back in the office tomorrow. Everyone very sympathetic. Even Francine called, but when she found that the injuries were essentially superficial and limited to what is laughingly called "cuts and abrasions" she hung up.

September 29: I do not know how I feel about the beggar, now that he has beaten me. Today, driven by an impulse I could not understand, I visited him in the security ward where he is being held for observation. He made no attempt to escape after the beating, merely standing over me and muttering strange threats while the large crowd which had gathered parted for the police to take him easily. "Why?" I asked him through the little window; "why did you do it? I would have given you money. I would have . . ." In my mouth are the words: *I would have given you anything if you had asked; I thought you were the Saviour,* but I do not say them. After all, I am in a mental hospital, our conversation monitored. Also, I am not sure that I believe this any more. Everything that has happened to me in the last months, everything that I was thinking, seems to have been a strange illness that was battered from me; not only my blood but convictions poured on the stones. "Why?" I said again weakly.

The beggar said nothing. His eyes cold and empty, his hands rigid on the panels, his body a withdrawal. Nothing, nothing. Is it possible that he was a simple lunatic from the beginning, the beating merely because I became a focus by our constant interception of paths? Or has something gone away from him; that which I suspected never to be touched?

It does not matter. I left, telling the authorities on the way out that no, I would not press charges if the beggar were confined for a long, long time.

No rising, no fire, no music, no thousand years of destruction. Only this grey inelegance, but looking through the trap of choices, I see that it could have been no other way. We are not for the quick-fire.

September 30: The President was shot in the shoulder while leaving a press-conference. The assailant has been seized; a foreigner from the East protesting the President's policy of non-involvement in the war. He seems barely coherent but is perhaps merely excited. The shot narrowly missed the President's temple at close range, but due to the fortunate escape, he is expected to be back at his desk within the week. Already he is conducting business from his hospital bed and has released a statement to the nation calling for calm.

Another call from Francine tonight, sounding much calmer herself, as if the near-assassination had deeply touched her. She said she felt guilty in some way for my severe beating and wondered if somehow, some way, we could make another try at our marriage.

I told her that we would see. Tonight, she is supposed to spend the evening with me. The thoughts are less tormenting than they have been for months and I think that I may, if circumstances turn a certain way, be able to function. I want to function; it is the least that I could do in line with the gravity of events and with the President's appeal.

October 14: Only a few weeks but September seems so far from me now. A different world; an enclosure from which I have been sprung. Francine has come back to live with me; my work is becoming meaningful again, the word from the networks and newspapers merely uncomfortable but no longer signs and portents. The beggar has been found insane and remanded upstate. It does not seem to have happened. Reality has once again overtaken me; joyfully I will confront it.

This morning, at the agency, working on skewed responses in Dayton to the President's quick and astonishing recovery, I thought once again that I saw a vision of the Coming but it was not as it had been before and not as it had ever been in my life. Looking at the charts, the figures, the slow curves being traced out, I thought I saw in that lovely coldness, entrapped in peace forever, the face of the Saviour, and the joy that I felt as I moved the pencil to capture the details, the vaulting of the heart as I saw him pure before me in the forty-seven percent of Dayton that no longer accepts the teachings of any Church . . . this arc of happiness took me like grace and falling all the way down, I sung the sound of Gabriel.

in this sign

BY RAY BRADBURY

Fire exploded over summer night lawns. You saw sparkling faces of uncles and aunts. Skyrockets fell up in the brown shining eyes of cousins on the porch, and the cold charred sticks thumped down in dry meadows far away.

The Most Reverend Father Joseph Daniel Peregrine opened his eyes. What a dream: he and his cousins with their fiery play at his grandfather's ancient Ohio home so many years ago!

He lay listening to the great hollow of the church, the other cells where other Fathers lay. Had they, too, on the eve of the flight of the rocket *Crucifix*, lain with memories of the Fourth of July? Yes. This was like those breathless Independence dawns when you waited for the first concussion and rushed out on the dewy sidewalks, your hands full of loud miracles.

So here they were, the Episcopal Fathers, in the breathing dawn before they pinwheeled off to Mars, leaving their incense through the velvet cathedral of space.

"Should we go at all?" whispered Father Peregrine. "Shouldn't we solve our own sins on Earth? Aren't we running from our lives here?"

He rose, his fleshy body, with its rich look of strawberries, milk, and steak, moving heavily.

"Or is it sloth?" he wondered. "Do I dread the journey?"

He stepped into the needle-spray shower.

"But I shall take you to Mars, body." He addressed himself. "Leaving old sins here. And on to Mars to find *new* sins?" A delightful thought, almost. Sins no one had ever thought of. Oh, he himself had written a little book. *The Problem of Sin on Other Worlds*, ignored as somehow not serious enough by his Episcopal brethren.

Only last night, over a final cigar, he and Father Stone had talked of it.

"On Mars, sin might appear as virtue. We must guard against virtuous acts there that later might be found to be sins!" said Father Peregrine, beaming. "How exciting. It's been centuries since so much adventure has accompanied the prospect of being a missionary!"

"*I* will recognize sin," said Father Stone, bluntly, "*even* on Mars."

"Oh, we priests pride ourselves on being litmus paper, changing color in sin's presence," retorted Father Peregrine, "but what if Martian chemistry is such that we do not color *at all!* If there are new senses on Mars, you must admit the possibility of unrecognizable sin."

"If there is no malice aforethought, there is no sin or punishment for same, the Lord assures us that," Father Stone replied.

"On Earth, yes. But perhaps a Martian sin might inform the subconscious of its evil, telepathically, leaving the conscious mind of man free to act, seemingly without malice! What *then?*"

"What *could* there be in the way of new sins?"

Father Peregrine leaned heavily forward. "Adam *alone* did not sin. Add Eve and you add temptation. Add a second man and you make adultery possible. With the addition of sex or people, you add sin. If men were harmless they could not strangle with their hands. You would not have that particular sin of murder. Add arms, and you add the possibility of a new violence. Amoebas cannot sin because they reproduce by fission. They do not covet wives or murder each other. Add sex to amoebas, and arms and legs, and you would have murder and adultery. Add an arm or a leg to persons, or take away each, and you add or subtract possible evil. On Mars, what if there are five new senses, organs, invisible limbs we can't conceive of, then mightn't there be five *new sins!*"

Father Stone gasped. "I think you *enjoy* this sort of thing!"

"I keep my mind alive, Father, just alive, is all."

"Your mind's always juggling, isn't it; mirrors, torches, plates?"

"Yes. Because sometimes the Church seems like those posed circus tableaux where the curtain lifts and men, white, zinc-oxide, talcum-powder statues, freeze to represent abstract Beauty. Very wonderful. But I hope there will always be room for me to dart about between the statues, don't you, Father Stone?"

Father Stone had moved away. "I think we'd better go to bed. In a few hours we'll be jumping up to see your *new* sins, Father Peregrine."

The rocket stood ready for the firing.

The Fathers walked from their devotions in the chilly morning, many a fine priest from New York or Chicago or Los Angeles—the Church was sending its best—walking across town to the frosty field. Walking, Father Peregrine remembered the Bishop's words:

"Father Peregrine, you will captain the missionaries, with Father Stone at your side. Having chosen you for this serious task, I find my reasons deplorably obscure, Father, but your pamphlet on planetary sin did not go unread. You are a flexible man. And Mars is like that uncleaned closet we have neglected for millenniums. Sin has collected there like bric-a-brac. Mars is twice Earth's age and has had double the number of Saturday nights, liquor baths, and eye-poppings at women as naked as white seals. When we open that closet door, things will fall on us. We need a quick, flexible man, one whose mind can dodge. Anyone a little too dogmatic might break in two. I feel you'll be resilient. Father, the job is yours."

The Bishop and the Fathers knelt.

The blessing was said and the rocket given a little shower of holy water. Arising, the Bishop addressed them:

"I know you will go with God, to prepare the Martians for the reception of His Truth. I wish you all a *thoughtful* journey."

They filed past the Bishop, twenty men, robes whispering, to deliver their hands into his kind hands before passing into the cleansed projectile.

"I wonder," said Father Peregrine, at the last moment, "if Mars is hell? Only waiting for our arrival before it bursts into brimstone and fire."

"Lord, be with us," said Father Stone.

The rocket moved.

Coming out of space was like coming out of the most beautiful cathedral they had ever seen. Touching Mars was like touching the ordinary pavement outside the church five minutes after having *really* known your love for God.

The Fathers stepped gingerly from the steaming rocket and knelt upon Martian sand while Father Peregrine gave thanks.

"Lord, we thank Thee for the journey through Thy rooms. And Lord, we have reached a new land, so we must have new eyes. We shall hear new sounds and must needs have new ears. And there will be new sins, for which we ask the gift of better and firmer and purer hearts. Amen."

They arose.

And here was Mars like a sea under which they trudged in the guise of submarine biologists, seeking life. Here the territory of hidden sin. Oh, how carefully they must all balance, like gray feathers, in this new element, afraid that walking *itself* might be sinful; or breathing, or simple fasting!

And here was the Mayor of First Town come to meet them with outstretched hand. "What can I do for you, Father Peregrine?"

"We'd like to know about the Martians. For only if we know about them can we plan our church intelligently. Are they ten feet tall? We will build large doors. Are their skins blue or red or green? We must know when we put human figures in the stained glass, so we may use the right skin color. Are they heavy? We will build sturdy seats for them."

"Father," said the Mayor, "I don't think you should worry about the Martians. There are two races. One of them is pretty well dead. A few are in hiding. And the second race, well, they're not quite human."

"Oh?" Father Peregrine's heart quickened.

"They're round luminous globes of light, Father, living in those hills. Man or beast, who can say, but they act intelligently, I hear." The Mayor shrugged. "Of course, they're not men, so I don't think you'll care—"

"On the contrary," said Father Peregrine swiftly. "Intelligent, you say?"

"There's a story. A prospector broke his leg in those hills, and would have died there. The blue spheres of light came at him. When he woke, he was down on a highway, and didn't know how he got there."

"Drunk," said Father Stone.

"That's the story," said the Mayor. "Father Peregrine, with most of the Martians dead, and only these Blue Spheres, I frankly think you'd be better off in First City. Mars is opening up. It's a frontier now, like in the old days on Earth, out west, and in Alaska. Men are pouring up here. There are a couple thousand black Irish mechanics and miners and day-laborers in First City who need saving, because there are too many wicked women who came with them, and too much ten-century-old Martian wine—"

Father Peregrine was gazing into the soft blue hills.

Father Stone cleared his throat. "Well, Father?"

Father Peregrine did not hear. "Spheres of blue *fire?*"

"Yes, Father."

"Ah," Father Peregrine sighed.

"Blue balloons." Father Stone shook his head. "A circus!"

Father Peregrine felt his wrists pounding. He saw the little frontier town with raw, fresh-built sin; and he saw the hills, old with the oldest and yet perhaps an even newer, to him, sin.

"Mayor . . . could your black Irish laborers cook one more day in hellfire?"

"I'd turn and baste them for you, Father."

Father Peregrine nodded to the hills. "Then, that's where we'll go."

There was a murmur from everyone.

"It would be so simple," explained Father Peregrine, "to go into town. I prefer to think that if the Lord walked here and people said, 'Here is the beaten path,' He would reply, 'Show me the weeds. I will *make* a path.'"

"But—"

"Father Stone, think how it would weigh upon us if we passed sinners by and did not extend our hands."

"But globes of fire!"

"I imagine man looked funny to other animals when he first appeared. Yet he has a soul, for all his homeliness. Until we prove otherwise, let us assume that these fiery spheres have souls."

"All right," agreed the Mayor, "but you'll be back to town."

"We'll see. First, some breakfast. Then you and I, Father Stone, will walk alone into the hills. I don't want to frighten those fiery Martians with machines or crowds. Shall we have breakfast?"

The Fathers ate in silence.

At nightfall, Father Peregrine and Father Stone were high in the hills. They stopped and sat upon a rock to enjoy a moment of relaxation and waiting. The Martians had not as yet appeared and they both felt vaguely disappointed.

"I wonder—" Father Peregrine mopped his face. "Do you think if we called 'Hello!' they might answer?"

"Father Peregrine, won't you ever be serious?"

"Not until the good Lord is. Oh, don't look so terribly shocked, please. The Lord is not serious. In fact, it is a little hard to know just what else He is except loving. And love has to do with humor, doesn't it? For you cannot love someone unless you put up with him, can you? And you cannot put up with someone constantly unless you can laugh at him, isn't that true? And certainly we are ridiculous little animals wallowing in the fudge-bowl, and God must love us all the more because we appeal to His humor."

"I never thought of God as humorous," said Father Stone, coldly.

"The Creator of the platypus, the camel, the ostrich, and Man? Oh, come now!" Father Peregrine laughed.

But at this instant, from among the twilight hills, like a series of blue lamps lit to guide their way, came the Martians.

Father Stone saw them first. "Look!"

Father Peregrine turned and the laughter stopped in his mouth.

The round blue globes of fire hovered among the twinkling stars, distantly trembling.

"Monsters!" Father Stone leaped up. But Father Peregrine caught him. "Wait!"

"We should've gone to town!"

"No, listen, look!" pleaded Father Peregrine.

"I'm afraid!"

"Don't be, this is God's work!"

"The devil's!"

"No, now quiet!" Father Peregrine gentled him and they crouched with the soft blue light on their upturned faces as the fiery orbs drew near.

And again, Independence Night, thought Father Peregrine trem-
oring. He felt like a child back in those July Fourth evenings, the sky
blowing apart, breaking into powdery stars and burning sound, the
concussions jingling house windows like the ice on a thousand thin
ponds. The aunts, uncles, cousins, crying Ah! as to some celestial physi-
cian. The summer sky colors. And the Fire Balloons, lit by an indulgent
Grandfather, steadied in his massively tender hands. Oh, the memory
of those lovely Fire Balloons, softly lighted, warmly billowed bits of
tissue, like insect wings, lying like folder wasps in boxes and, last of all,
after the day of riot and fury, at long last from their boxes, delicately
unfolded, blue, red, white, patriotic, the Fire Balloons!

He saw the dim faces of dear relatives long dead and mantled with
moss as Grandfather lit the tiny candle and let the warm air breathe up
to form the balloon plumply luminous in his hands, a shining vision
which they held, reluctant to let it go, for once released it was yet
another year gone from life, another Fourth, another bit of Beauty
vanished. And then up, up, still up through the warm summer night
constellations, the Fire Balloons had drifted, while red-white-and-blue
eyes followed them, wordless, from family porches. Away into deep
Illinois country, over night rivers and sleeping mansions the Fire Balloons dwindled, forever gone . . .

Father Peregrine felt tears in his eyes. Above him, the Martians,
not one but a *thousand* whispering Fire Balloons it seemed. Any moment, he might find his long dead and blessed Grandfather at his elbow,
staring up at Beauty.

But it was Father Stone.

"Let's go, please, Father!"

"I must speak to them." Father Peregrine rustled forward, not
knowing what to say, for what had he ever said to the Fire Balloons of
time past, except with his mind: *you are beautiful, you are beautiful,* and
that was not enough now. He could only lift his heavy arms and call
upward, as he had often wished to call after the enchanted Fire Balloons,
"Hello!"

But the fiery spheres only burnt like images in a dark mirror. They
seemed fixed, gaseous, miraculous, forever.

"We come with God," said Father Peregrine to the sky.

"Silly, silly, silly." Father Stone chewed the back of his hand. "In the name of God, Father Peregrine, stop!"

But now the phosphorescent spheres blew away into the hills. In a moment, they were gone.

Father Peregrine called again, and the echo of his last cry shook the hills above. Turning, he saw an avalanche shake out dust, pause, and then with a thunder of stone wheels, crash down the mountain upon them.

"Look what you've done!" cried Father Stone.

Father Peregrine was almost fascinated, then horrified. He turned, knowing they could run only a few feet before the rocks crushed them into ruins. He had time to whisper, *Oh, Lord!* and the rocks fell!

"Father!"

They were separated like chaff from wheat. There was a blue shimmering of globes, a shift of cold stars, a roar, and then they stood upon a ledge two hundred feet away watching the spot where their bodies should have been buried under tons of stone.

The blue light evaporated.

The two Fathers clutched each other. "What happened?"

"The blue fires lifted us!"

"We ran, *that* was it!"

"No, the globes saved us."

"They couldn't!"

"They *did.*"

The sky was empty. There was a feel as if a great bell had just stopped tolling. Reverberations lingered in their teeth and marrows.

"Let's get away from here. You'll have us killed."

"I haven't feared death for a good many years, Father Stone."

"We've proved nothing. Those blue lights ran off at the first cry. It's useless."

"No." Father Peregrine was suffused with a stubborn wonder. "Somehow, they saved us. That proves they have souls."

"It proves only that they *might* have saved us. Everything was confused. We might have escaped, ourselves."

"They are not animals, Father Stone. Animals do not save lives; especially of strangers. There is mercy and compassion here. Perhaps, tomorrow, we may prove more."

"Prove what? How?" Father Stone was immensely tired now, the outrage to his mind and body showed on his stiff face. "Follow them in helicopters, reading chapter and verse? They're not human. They haven't eyes or ears or bodies like ours."

"But I feel something about them," replied Father Peregrine. "I know a great revelation is at hand. They saved us. They *think*. They had a choice, let us live or die. That proves free will!"

Father Stone set to work building a fire, glaring at the sticks in his hands, choking on the grey smoke. "I myself will open a convent for nursing geese, a monastery for sainted swine, and I shall build a miniature apse in a microscope so that paramecia can attend services and tell their beads with their flagella."

"Oh, Father Stone,"

"I'm sorry." Father Stone blinked redly across the fire. "But this is like blessing a crocodile before he chews you up. You're risking the entire missionary expedition. We belong in First Town, washing liquor from men's throats and perfume off their hands!"

"Can't you recognize the human in the inhuman?"

"I'd much rather recognize the inhuman in the human."

"But if I prove these things sin, *know* sin, know a moral life, have free will and intellect, Father Stone?"

"That will take much convincing."

The night grew rapidly cold, and they peered into the fire to find their wildest thoughts while eating biscuits and berries, and soon they were bundled for sleep under the chiming stars. And just before turning one last time, Father Stone, who had been thinking for many minutes to find something to bother Father Peregrine about, stared into the soft pink charcoal bed and said, "No Adam and Eve on Mars. No original sin. Maybe the Martians live in a state of God's grace. Then we can go back down to town and start work on the Earth men."

Father Peregrine reminded himself to say a little prayer for Father Stone. "Yes, Father Stone, but there've been an Original Sin and a Martian Adam and Eve. We'll find them. Men are men, unfortunately, no matter what their shape, and inclined to sin."

But Father Stone was pretending sleep.

Father Peregrine did not shut his eyes.

Of course they couldn't let these Martians go to hell, could they? With a compromise to their consciences, could they go back to the new colonial towns, those towns so full of sinful gullets and women with scintilla eyes and white oyster bodies rollicking in beds with lonely laborers? Wasn't that the place for the Fathers? Wasn't this trek into the hills merely a personal whim? Was he really thinking of God's Church, or was he quenching the thirst of a sponge-like curiosity? Those blue round globes of St. Anthony's fire. How they burned in his mind! What a challenge, to find the man behind the mask, the human behind the inhuman. Wouldn't he be proud if he could say, even to his secret self, that he had converted a rolling huge pool table full of fiery spheres! What a sin of pride! Worth doing penance for! But then one did many prideful things out of Love, and he loved the Lord so much and was so happy at it that he wanted everyone else to be happy, too.

The last thing he saw before sleep was the return of the blue fires, like a flight of burning angels silently singing him to his worried rest.

The blue round dreams were still there in the sky when Father Peregrine awoke in the early morning.

Father Stone slept like a stiff bundle, quietly. Father Peregrine watched the Martians floating and watching him. They were human, he *knew* it. But he must prove it or face a dry-mouthed, dry-eyed Bishop telling him kindly to step aside.

But how to prove humanity if they hid in the high vaults of the sky? How to bring them nearer and provide answers to the many questions?

"They saved us from the avalanche."

Father Peregrine arose, moved off among the rocks, and began to climb the nearest hill, until he came to a place where a cliff dropped sheerly to a floor two hundred feet below. He was choking from the vigorous climb in the frosty air. He stood, getting his breath.

"If I fell from here, it would surely kill me."

He let a pebble drop. Moments later, it clicked on the rocks below.

"The Lord would never forgive me . . ."

He tossed another pebble.

"It wouldn't be suicide, would it, if I did it out of Love . . .?"

He lifted his gaze to the blue spheres. "But first, another try." He called to them. "Hello, hello!"

The echoes tumbled upon each other, but the blue fires did not blink or move.

He talked to them for five minutes. When he stopped, he peered and saw Father Stone, still indignantly asleep, below in the little camp.

"I must prove everything." Father Peregrine stepped to the cliff rim. "I am an old man. I am not afraid. Surely the Lord will understand that I am doing this for Him?"

He drew a deep breath. All his life swam through his eyes and he thought, In a moment, shall I die? I am afraid that I love living much too much. But I love other things more.

And thinking thus, he stepped off the cliff.

He fell.

"Fool!" he cried. He tumbled end over end. "You were wrong!" The rocks rushed up at him and he saw himself dashed on them and sent to glory. "Why did I do this thing?" But he knew the answer and an instant later was calm as he fell. The wind roared around him and the rocks hurtled to meet him.

And then there was a shift of stars, a glimmering of blue light, and he felt himself surrounded by blueness and suspended. A moment later he was deposited, with a gentle bump, upon the rocks, where he sat a full moment, alive, and touching himself and looking up at those blue lights that had withdrawn instantly.

"You saved me!" he whispered. "You wouldn't let me die. You knew it was wrong."

He rushed over to Father Stone who was still quietly asleep. "Father, Father, wake up!" He shook at him and brought him around. "Father, they saved me!"

"Who saved you?" Father Stone blinked and sat up.

Father Peregrine related his experience.

"A dream, a nightmare, go back to sleep," said Father Stone, irritably. "You and your circus balloons."

"But I was awake!"

"Now, now, Father, calm yourself, there now."

"You don't believe me? Have you a gun, yes, there, let me have it."

"What are you going to do?" Father Stone handed over the small pistol they had brought along for protection against snakes or other similar and unpredictable animals.

Father Peregrine seized the pistol. "I'll prove it!"

He pointed the pistol at his own hand and fired.

"Stop!"

There was a shimmer of light and before their eyes, the bullet stood upon the air, poised an inch from his open palm. It hung for a moment, surrounded by a blue phosphorescence. Then it fell, hissing, into the dust.

Father Peregrine fired the gun three times, at his hand, at his leg, at his body. The three bullets hovered, glittering, and like dead insects, fell at their feet.

"You see?" said Father Peregrine, letting his arm fall, and allowing the pistol to drop after the bullets. "They know. They understand. They are not animals. They think and judge and live in a moral climate. What animal would save me from myself like this? There is no animal would do that. Only another man, Father. Now, do you believe?"

Father Stone was watching the sky and the blue lights, and now, silently, he dropped to one knee and picked up the warm bullets and cupped them in his hand. He closed his hand tight.

The sun was rising behind them.

"I think we had better go down to the others and tell them of this and bring them back up here," said Father Peregrine.

By the time the sun was up, they were well on their way back to the rocket.

Father Peregrine drew the round circle in the center of the blackboard.

"This is Christ, the Son of the Father."

He pretended not to hear the other Fathers' sharp intake of breath.

"This is Christ, in all His Glory," he continued.

"It looks like a geometry problem," observed Father Stone.

"A fortunate comparison, for we deal with symbols here. Christ is no less Christ, you must admit, in being represented by a circle or a square. For centuries the cross has symbolized His love and agony. So, this circle will be the Martian Christ. This is how we shall bring Him to Mars."

The Fathers stirred fretfully and looked at each other.

"You, Brother Mathias, will create, in glass, a replica of this circle, a globe, filled with bright fire. It will stand upon the altar."

"A cheap magic trick," muttered Father Stone.

Father Peregrine went on patiently. "On the contrary. We are giving them God in an understandable image. If Christ had come to us on Earth as an octopus, would we have accepted Him readily?" He spread his hands. "Was it then a cheap magic trick of the Lord's to bring us Christ through Jesus in man's shape? After we bless the church we build here and sanctify its altar and this symbol, do you think Christ would refuse to inhabit the shape before us? You know in your hearts He would not refuse."

"But the body of a soulless animal!" said Brother Mathias.

"We've already gone over that, many times since we returned this morning, Brother Mathias. These creatures saved us from the avalanche. They realized that self-destruction was sinful, and prevented it, time after time. Therefore we must build a church in the hills, live with them to find their own special ways of sinning, the alien ways, and help them."

The Fathers did not seem cheered at the prospect.

"Is it because they are so odd to the eye?" wondered Father Peregrine. "But what is a shape? Only a cup for the blazing soul that God provides us all. If tomorrow I found that sea-lions suddenly possessed free will, intellect, knew when not to sin, knew what life was and tempered justice with mercy and life with love, then I would build an undersea cathedral. And if the sparrows should miraculously, with God's will, gain everlasting souls tomorrow, I would freight a church with helium and take after them, for all souls, in the shape, if they have free will and are aware of their sins, will burn in hell unless given their rightful communions. I would not let a Martian sphere burn in hell, either, for it is a sphere only in mine eyes. When I close my eyes it stands before me, an intelligence, a love, a soul, and I must not deny it."

"But that glass globe you wish placed on the altar," protested Father Stone.

"Consider the Chinese," replied Father Peregrine, imperturbably. "What sort of Christ do Christian Chinese worship? An Oriental Christ, naturally. You've all seen Oriental Nativity scenes. How is Christ dressed? In Eastern robes. Where does He walk? In Chinese settings of bamboo and misty mountain and crooked tree. His eyelids taper, His cheekbones rise. Each country, each race adds something to our Lord. I am reminded of the Virgin of Guadalupe, to whom all Mexico pays its love. Her skin? Have you noticed the paintings of her? A dark skin, like that of her worshippers. Is this blasphemy? Not at all. It is not logical that men should accept a God, no matter how real, of another color. I often wonder why our missionaries do well in Africa, with a snow-white Christ. Perhaps because white is a sacred color, in albino, or any other form, to the African tribes. Given time, mightn't Christ darken there, too? The form does not matter. Content is everything. We cannot expect these Martians to accept an alien form. We shall give them Christ in their own image."

"There's a flaw in your reasoning, Father," said Father Stone. "Won't the Martians suspect us of hypocrisy? They will realize that *we* don't worship a round, globular Christ, but a man with limbs and a head. How do we explain the difference?"

"By showing there is none. Christ will fill any vessel that is offered. Bodies or globes, He is there, and each will worship the same thing in a different guise. What is more, we must *believe* in this globe we give the Martians. We must believe in a shape which is meaningless to us as to form. This spheroid *will* be Christ. And we must remember that we ourselves, and the shape of our Earth Christ, would be meaningless, ridiculous, a squander of material to these Martians."

Father Peregrine laid aside his chalk. "Now, let us go into the hills and build our church."

The Fathers began to pack their equipment.

The church was not a church but an area cleared of rocks, a plateau on one of the low mountains, its soil smoothed and brushed, and an altar established whereon Brother Mathias placed the fiery globe he had constructed.

At the end of six days of work the "church" was ready.

"What shall we do with this?" Father Stone tapped an iron bell they had brought along. "What does a bell mean to *them*."

"I imagine I brought it for our own comfort," admitted Father Peregrine. "We need a few familiarities. This church seems so little like a church. And we feel somewhat absurd here, even I, for it is something new, this business of converting the creatures of another world. I feel like a ridiculous play-actor at times. And then I pray to God to lend me strength."

"Many of the Fathers are unhappy. Some of them joke about all this, Father Peregrine."

"I know. We'll put this bell in a small tower for their comfort, anyway."

"What about the organ?"

"We'll play it at the first service, tomorrow."

"But, the Martians—"

"I know. But again, I suppose, for our own comfort, our own music. Later, we may discover theirs."

They rose very early on Sunday morning and moved through the coldness like pale phantoms, rime tinkling on their habits; covered with chimes they were, shaking down showers of silver water.

"I wonder if it *is* Sunday here on Mars?" mused Father Peregrine, but seeing Father Stone wince, hastened on, "It might be Tuesday or Thursday, who knows? But no matter. My idle fancy. It's Sunday to *us*. Come."

The Fathers walked into the flat wide area of the "church" and knelt, shivering, and blue-lipped.

Father Peregrine said a little prayer and put his cold fingers to the organ keys. The music went up like a flight of pretty birds. He touched the keys like a man moving his hands among the weeds of a wild garden, startling up great soarings of beauty into the hills.

The music calmed the air. It smelled the fresh smell of morning. The music drifted into the mountains and shook down mineral powders in a dusty rain.

The Fathers waited.

"Well, Father Peregrine." Father Stone eyed the empty sky where the sun was rising, furnace-red. "I don't see our friends."

"Let me try again." Father Peregrine was perspiring.

He built an architecture of Bach, stone by exquisite stone, raising a music cathedral so vast that its furthest chancels were in Nineveh, its furthest dome at St. Peter's left hand. The music stayed and did not crash in ruin when it was over, but partook of a series of white clouds and was carried away among other lands.

The sky was still empty.

"They'll come!" But Father Peregrine felt the panic in his chest, very small, growing. "Let us pray. Let us ask them to come. They read minds; they *know.*"

The Fathers lowered themselves yet again, in rustlings and whispers. They prayed.

And to the East, out of the icy mountains of seven o'clock on Sunday morning or perhaps Thursday morning or maybe Monday morning on Mars, came the soft fiery globes.

They hovered and sank and filled the area around the shivering priests. "Thank you, oh thank you, Lord." Father Peregrine shut his eyes tight and played the music and when it was done he turned and gazed upon his wondrous congregation.

And a voice touched his mind, and the voice said:

"We have come for a little while."

"You may stay," said Father Peregrine.

"For a little while only," said the voice, quietly. "We have come to tell you certain things. We should have spoken sooner. But we had hoped that you might go on your way if left alone."

Father Peregrine started to speak, but the voice hushed him.

"We are the Old Ones," the voice said, and it entered him like a blue, gaseous flare and burned in the chambers of his head. "We are the old Martians, who left our marble cities and went into the hills, forsaking the material life we had lived. So very long ago we became these things that we now are. Once, we were men, with bodies and legs and arms such as yours. The legend has it that one of us, a good man, discovered a way to free man's soul and intellect, to free him of bodily ills and melancholies, or deaths and transfigurations, of ill humors and senilities, and so we took on the look of lightning and blue fire and have lived in the winds and skies and hills forever after that, neither prideful nor arrogant, neither rich nor poor, passionate or cold. We have lived apart from those we left behind, those other men of this world, and how we came to be has been forgotten, the process lost, but we shall never die, nor do harm. We have put away the sins of the body and live in God's grace. We covet no other property, we have no property, we do not steal, nor kill, nor lust, nor hate. We live in happiness. We cannot reproduce, we do not eat or drink or make war. All the sensualities and childishness and sins of the body were stripped away when our bodies were put aside. We have left sin behind, Father Peregrine, and it is burned like the leaves in the autumn wicker and it is gone like the soiled snow of an evil winter, and it is gone like the sexual flowers of a red and yellow spring, and it is gone like the panting nights of hottest summer, and our season is temperate and our clime is rich in thought."

Father Peregrine was standing now, for the voice touched him at such a pitch that it almost shook him from his senses. It was an ecstasy and a fire washing through him.

"We wish to tell you that we appreciate your building this place for us, but we have no need for it, for each of us is a temple unto himself, and needs no place wherein to cleanse himself. Forgive us for not coming to you sooner, but we are separate and apart and have talked to no one for ten thousand years, nor have we interfered in any way with the life of this planet. It has come into your mind now that we are the lilies of the field, we toil not, neither do we spin. You are right. And so we suggest that you take the parts of this temple into your own cities and there cleanse them. For, rest assured, we are happy and at peace."

The Fathers were on their knees in the vast blue light, and Father Peregrine was down, too, and they were weeping, and it did not matter that their time had been wasted, it did not matter to them at all.

The blue spheres murmured and began to rise once more, on a breath of cool air.

"May I—" cried Father Peregrine, not daring to ask, eyes closed. "May I come again, some day, that I may learn from you?"

The blue fires blazed. The air trembled.

Yes. Some day he might come again. Some day.

And then the Fire Balloons blew away and were gone, and he was like a child, on his knees, tears streaming from his eyes, crying to himself,

Come back! Come back! and at any moment Grandfather might lift him
and carry him upstairs to his bedroom in a long-gone Ohio town . . .

They filed down out of the hills at sunset. Looking back, Father
Peregrine saw the blue fires burning. No, he thought, we couldn't build
a church for the likes of you. You're Beauty itself. What church could
compete with the fireworks of the pure soul?

Father Stone moved in silence beside him. And at last he spoke:

"The way I see it is there's a Truth on every planet. All parts of
the Big Truth. On a certain day they'll all fit together like the pieces
of a jigsaw. This has been a shaking experience. I'll never doubt again,
Father Peregrine. For this Truth here is as true as Earth's Truth, and
they lie side by side. And we'll go on to other worlds, adding the sum
parts of the Truth until one day the whole Total will stand before us
like the light of a new day."

"That's a lot, coming from you, Father Stone."

"I'm sorry now, in a way, we're going down to the town to handle
our own kind. Those blue lights now, when they settled about us, and
that *voice.*" Father Stone shivered.

Father Peregrine reached out to take the other's arm. They
walked together.

"And you know," said Father Stone, finally, fixing his eyes on
Brother Mathias who strode ahead with the glass sphere tenderly carried
in his arms, that glass sphere with the blue phosphorus light glowing
forever inside it, "you know, Father Peregrine, that globe there—"

"Yes?"

"It's Him! It *is* Him, after all."

Father Peregrine smiled and they walked down out of the hills
toward the new town.

contributors

POUL ANDERSON, like Ray Bradbury, has been the recipient of numerous honors, including Nebula and Hugo awards. Among his recent titles are *The Queen of Air and Darkness* and *Orbit Unlimited*. Mr. Anderson is a former president of Science Fiction Writers of America. He is also a poet, critic, and nonfiction writer, and still somehow manages to find time to engage in medieval-style tournies.

RAY BRADBURY was born in 1920 and published his first short story in 1941. He has since established himself as an important and influential literary figure whose many works include the now-classic *Dandelion Wine*. He lives in Los Angeles, California, where he gets around by bicycle.

PHILIP JOSÉ FARMER, veteran science fiction author, recently published *Doc Savage: His Apocalyptic Life*. He writes biography and nonfiction in addition to science fiction, and is currently editing a collection of pieces dealing in different ways with the idea—and occasional fact—of humans nurtured by animals.

EDWARD HOCH is a frequent contributor to mystery magazines, a member of Mystery Writers of America, and editor of *Dear Dead Days: The Mystery Writers of America 1972 Anthology*. His *Fellowship of the Hand* was published in 1973. He and his wife live in Rochester, New York, where he was born in 1930.

JOAN C. HOLLY, "a science fiction writer's science fiction writer," is at work on a novel which her compeers await with as much eagerness as the audience her short stories have attracted.

K. M. O'DONNELL is the pseudonym for one of the most popular—and prolific—science fiction writers of today. Together, he and his alter ego can claim more than sixty novels and over a hundred short stories. In his incarnation as O'Donnell, he is the author of *Final War*, and, more recently, *Universe Day*.

5927 / 63
199